MW00768622

ISLAND AUTUMN

To Amy—
Best wishes!

ISLAND AUTUMN

A Seacoast Island Romance: Volume 2

JESSICA RANDOLPH

Jessica

This is a work of fiction. Names, characters, places, and incidents
are the products of the author's imagination or are used fictitiously.
Any resemblance to actual events, locales, or persons, living or
dead, is entirely coincidental.

Copyright ©2015 by Jessica Randolph
All rights reserved.

ISBN-13: 9781519101655

1

"You're kidding me," Morgan Bailey said into the phone, as a cold sweat broke out on her forehead.

The woman on the other end of the line sniffed. "Probably'll be six months this time." She was Morgan's contractor's wife. "Possession and all that."

"But he swore he'd have my roof finished by October first. And it's September twenty-first today! What am I going to do? Do you know anyone who can finish it for me?"

"No, I don't. But if you'd send me the money you owe him, I'd sure appreciate it."

"All he did was rip off the shingles and set up the scaffolding, and now I'm up a creek and he's in jail!"

"You at least owe for the hours he worked."

"Fine, whatever," Morgan said, and hung up. Her hand was shaking.

Her best friend, Lainey, who was sitting at Morgan's kitchen counter, hands wrapped around a steaming mug, raised her eyebrows. "Jail?" Lainey had stopped over for a quick cup of tea, filling the narrow window of time between when Morgan finished serving breakfast to her guests and when Lainey opened her book and wine shop, which was just three doors down from Morgan's Seacoast Bed and Breakfast. Both properties looked out over a meadow filled with wildflowers that spilled down to the harbor of Seacoast Island, Maine, which had been Morgan's home for the last six years, ever since her husband, Rick, a Marine, had been killed in Afghanistan, leaving her with a hollower heart than she'd ever imagined possible. All the insurance money had gone into purchasing and renovating her B&B, which kept her so busy most of the year that she hardly had time to think. Which was just the way she wanted it.

Morgan jabbed the START button on the coffee maker; it whirred and dribbled. "For Pete's sake. Couldn't the guy have at least waited till *after* he had my roof done to get arrested? He's been putting me off all summer, putting other jobs ahead of mine, and he *knew* how important this was to me. I've got that person from *Simple Food* coming to judge my three breakfasts and take photos, and I won't win *anything* if I've got no roof and all this scaffolding set up all around. And she's coming in only three weeks! Not to mention, God knows where all the roof'll leak, without shingles on. The guy told me the only reason he was leaving it over the weekend was because the forecast was clear. What if I can't get it done by *winter*?"

Lainey looked as worried as Morgan felt. "There has to be *someone* who can finish it for you."

"Who? Your husband's got the only carpenter out here so tied up he'll have to work double-time till the snow flies to finish everything." Seeing Lainey's mouth start to open, Morgan held up a hand. "And, before you

2

say anything, no, I wouldn't dream of taking him away from Brick. Besides, he probably doesn't have roofing experience."

Lainey's new husband had come to Seacoast Island from Boston last summer with a building project in mind, then ended up falling for Lainey – and for the island as it was – instead. An architect, he'd spent the last year-plus designing upgrades to several traditional buildings on the island to make them more energy efficient. He never could find enough workers to do everything he had planned, especially since the ferry schedule meant that anyone who worked on the island pretty much had to live there, too, at least if they wanted to work more than a few hours a day. Morgan had the advantage of having a couch to offer in the den off her bedroom on the first floor. She hadn't been crazy about having the roofer sleeping in there last week, but that had seemed the only way to get the project done. If only she'd stopped him when he'd wanted to go home to the mainland for the weekend.

Lainey's brow furrowed. "Well, who, then? Everyone's got their hands more than full, this time of year."

"Tell me about it. Even if I knew what I was doing, which I don't, *I* wouldn't even have time, what with my guests and the garden and perfecting my recipes. Not to mention getting the rest of the place ship-shape. Twenty-five percent of the score is determined by 'overall experience.' If I don't get the roof on and the scaffolding down, that editor who surprised me this spring will be furious. He evidently really had to go to bat for me. His publisher thought it'd be better to have a more accessible location representing New England, but that editor had loved my cookbook so much that he convinced him."

Four years ago, after only a couple seasons running the Seacoast B&B, Morgan had self-published *COOKING BREAKAST FOR A CROWD: Notes from a Seacoast Island Innkeeper.* She'd imagined it as a souvenir some guests might like to take home, plus a way for her to bring in extra income. It had sold twenty thousand copies, mostly in the first two years. One had made it onto the desk of an editor of *Simple Food* – which, in turn, had brought him to her doorstep this past June. She hadn't known who he was when she'd served him and his wife their meals over their three-day stay; two weeks later, she'd gotten an email stating she was a finalist in their "Best B&B Breakfasts" contest. Ten B&Bs, two from each region of the country – New England, East, South, Midwest, and West – had been chosen. Five would be named best in their region, and one would be awarded "Best Overall" – and a grand prize of $10,000.

"Can't you just *submit* a photo?" Lainey said.

Morgan shook her head. "The only photos they'll use are ones the judge takes on the visit. Besides, imagine trying to cook for this judge with the roof leaking all over the place. Boy, with every day that passes, I only hate Woods and Water more!" This past winter, a couple from New Jersey had appeared on the island with a work crew of their own, thrown up a massive new "cottage" in record time, and, in June, opened the Woods and Water B&B. It was gorgeous, and featured gas log fireplaces and private baths in each guest room, some with whirlpool tubs. Even Morgan's most loyal guests, who'd been staying with her for years and giving nothing but rave reviews, had begun musing on how nice a private bath would be. Right now, her three upstairs guest rooms had to share one – and a few couples this summer, on arriving and discovering the situation, had actually moved up to Woods and Water.

"*What* water?" Lainey joked. "They've got no view at all up there. Besides, everybody says their breakfasts are hardly a step above Denny's. And evidently the husband never comes out of his painting studio, so the place has this weird artist-in-the-attic feel, and the wife is so intense people can't wait to get out of there in the mornings. I never see them around town, do you? They must have their food and supplies delivered."

"I know," Morgan said, "but some of my repeat customers have gone M.I.A. I think they're actually making next year's reservations up there. Just for the bathrooms! And the guest rooms are bigger, too, and everything's brand new. I've just got to finish this roof in time. Even if I don't win the grand prize, think of the new business that being featured would bring. I could probably even extend my season. Either way, I could put in private bathrooms."

Lainey stood. "Listen, I'll talk to Brick and see if he has any ideas."

"Great. I'll start making calls to the mainland."

Lainey smiled encouragingly. "We'll get this figured out."

Morgan grinned, poured herself a cup of coffee. "Fueled by caffeine, empowered by Google, that's me." She waved goodbye to Lainey and sat down at her computer, glad, as always, that she'd invested in high-speed satellite internet this past spring. Mentally crossing her fingers, wiping the sweat from her face, she clicked to open her browser and typed MAINE ROOFERS.

By five o'clock, Morgan had talked to seventeen roofing companies and twenty independent contractors from all over the state of Maine. Most were booked up through the winter. Two said they might be able to squeeze her in between other jobs, but once she'd described how she'd need them to come as soon as possible and stay on the island until they got the job done, they'd reconsidered. "Lady, you're asking for the moon," one told her. Then Lainey called and said Brick had tried a few people and struck out, too.

Morgan hung up the phone and did the same thing she always did when she was desperate or felt alone with her problems. She talked, in her mind, to her late husband. Maybe it was crazy, but it always made her feel better. She'd imagine him smiling, kissing her forehead and telling her not to worry. "Everything's going to be fine," she'd all but hear him say, same as he had – even if it was just over the phone from the Middle East – every single day starting the Valentine's Day they'd met in 2003 right up until the day in the summer of 2006 that he'd been killed. "I've got this," he'd say. "Don't you worry about a thing, babe."

Rick, what should I do?

Suddenly, she had an idea. That happened, sometimes: the minute she asked Rick what to do, she'd know. Again, maybe it was crazy to think he was communicating with her from beyond the grave, but – whatever worked.

She sat down at the computer again and logged on to her personal Facebook. "What's on my mind?" she said out loud. "Let me tell you." She typed: *Due to circumstances beyond my control, I am in DESPERATE need of someone to finish my roof in the next three weeks at LATEST. Rain and snow are coming and will equal disaster. Can any of you help, or do you know of anyone who can? I'd pay well for the work, plus for transportation, and will provide food and lodging, of course!* She wouldn't say it was just a couch. *P.M. me, please!!*

She clicked "Post" and sat back. The post popped up in her newsfeed. She waited. Stupid to think anything would happen immediately, but, still, she waited. First one, then two, then three people "liked" the post – what good did that do?

Suddenly, the computer pinged. A message! "*Sure, I can come.*"

"Thank God!" she said out loud, then she saw who the message was from. "Honestly?" she said, out loud again, this time talking to Rick. "Jesse Stewart?"

She got no answer, of course.

Her mind was whirling. Jesse Stewart. Rick's best friend from the Marines. Jesse Stewart, who hated her. Why would *he* volunteer to help? She'd forgotten they were even Facebook friends, forgotten he'd sent her a request years ago. She never saw any posts from him. How had he seen hers immediately?

The computer pinged. *"When do you need me?"*

She bit her lip, peering closely at the tiny picture next to the message of a ruggedly handsome guy about her age, grinning, wearing a straw cowboy hat, holding a guitar. Jesse Stewart – looking a few years older but just as good (this seemed unfortunate, and also unfair – why hadn't Rick had the chance to age well?) as the last time she'd seen him. Never mind that he was about her least favorite person in the world, a person she'd spent years trying not to think of. He'd been the one, she was sure, responsible for Rick's re-enlisting; by extension, for Rick's leaving her again for a third and final tour of duty.

She was sure she was one of Jesse's least favorite people, too, since he'd blamed *her* for breaking up his engagement, just because she'd seen his fiancée out with another man while Jesse and Rick were overseas. She clicked on his profile and saw his status was still "single" – surely Morgan hadn't ruined his love life for good?

Either way, she did not want to see Jesse Stewart. Or give him any chance to help her and look like he was some kind of good guy. Not even if he was the last man on earth with a hammer.

Of course, given her thirty-seven phone calls today, he kind of *was* the last man on earth with a hammer – at least, in her world, he might as well be. And, outside, the wind was kicking up. Rain and snow were on the way, no question.

"Really, sweetheart?" she said aloud to Rick, and got only silence in reply.

Okay, so Jesse Stewart was pretty much her only option. Beggars couldn't be choosers, right? She clicked on the message box and typed, *"Um, tomorrow?"* Surely there was no way, no way, he was actually going to agree. Where did he live, anyway? Wasn't he still in the Marines?

She looked at his profile. Worked at U.S. Marines and Stewart Contracting – his dad's business. So he was out. Living in his hometown (South View High, Class of 2002, according to his profile) of Fayetteville, North Carolina. Not so very far from Camp LeJeune, where they'd all been together, what seemed like a lifetime ago.

The computer was silent a full minute. Two. *He was just joking,* she thought. *Or someone else is on his account typing random messages to people.*

Then, a ping: *"Saturday work for you?"*

2

Jesse Stewart eased his old Ford pickup into a narrow parking space and cut off the engine and lights, casting the weathered fence in front of him and the mirrored surface of the water beyond into the shadow of the gray morning. The fog was so thick he'd hardly been able to see twenty feet in front of him the whole drive up here, and now on the water the shadowy forms of boats and buoys were barely distinguishable.

Yesterday morning, when he'd left Fayetteville, it had been a perfect, sunny eighty degrees. He'd driven till he could hardly see straight, eight hundred miles to Portsmouth, New Hampshire, then this morning all the way to this remote ferry stop in fifty degree, foggy, damp Maine. *Smart, Stewart, real smart, to give up that for* this, he thought, though of course he had a good reason for being here: that promise he'd made his best buddy Rick one night when they were half-drunk and talking about what-if-the-worst-happened. Jesse had told Rick he'd keep an eye on Morgan, help her if she needed it. Ever since the worst *had* happened to Rick, Jesse had hoped he could just fulfill that promise from a distance, like he'd been doing for six years now, keeping an eye on her Facebook profile, telling himself she seemed like she was doing just fine.

Then she'd sent out that cry for help the other day, and Jesse could all but hear Rick saying, "Uh, buddy? Remember?" So Jesse'd told his dad he needed some time off work – it wasn't like he couldn't spare him, since Jesse'd been out of the Marines and working for him only two months – and here he was.

He stepped out of the warm truck and started shivering right away, as he grabbed his things from behind the seat: duffel, guitar case, tool bag and belt. That was all he'd need. He slammed the door with a metallic thunk and adjusted his beat-up straw cowboy hat. A bell clanged in the distance across the smooth water. The ferry whistle blew.

He headed for the dock, not wanting to let anyone down or go back on his promises, but dreading seeing the woman who, the way he saw it, had basically ruined his life.

Inside the ferry, he dropped his guitar and duffel and tool belt onto the floor and sat on a bench nearby, unable to get warm after his brief exposure to the damp, raw cold. But being cold and wet went right along with the uncomfortable memories he couldn't stop replaying. Rick coming to him one night in their quarters in the desert, saying, "Buddy, bad news. Morgan saw Dawn at the Roper, dancing with some guy, getting real cozy. Kissing and so on. They left together."

Jesse had tried to laugh off the news, though in his gut he'd known it was true. The girl whose finger he'd put a ring on the minute he'd arrived home from his last deployment – the girl he'd spent every possible minute with before leaving again a few months later – had been sounding a little cagey every time he'd talked with her. He'd been planning to let sleeping dogs lie. He was confident he'd have her full attention once he got home; besides, focusing on the life that was waiting with her when he got back was what got him through the days in the desert. "You ever stop to think Morgan could be making that up, buddy?" he said to Rick. "God knows she doesn't like me."

"She wouldn't make up something like that. She's trying to watch out for you. Listen, you can't let Dawn get away with this."

Good old Rick, and good old Morgan. They always saw things in black and white. Expected everybody's love to be as pure-as-the-driven-snow as theirs. They never understood that the lives of regular people had gray areas. Serious ones.

Yet, over the next weeks, Morgan hadn't let up telling Rick about what Dawn was up to, and Rick hadn't let up telling Jesse that he had to confront Dawn. When Jesse finally did, that had been the end of that. With nothing to look forward to, and nobody sending him sweet messages of support to get him through the days and nights, Jesse fell into a funk, got into a fight with the captain, and consequently got transferred to another sector. And then Rick, whom Jesse had left behind, got blown up by an I.E.D., and Jesse was left completely alone, trying to puzzle out the gray areas, knowing he probably wouldn't have been able to save Rick even if he'd been there – but not quite believing it. Knowing that other things could have happened to ruin his vision of marrying Dawn, having babies, making a real life as a family – yet somehow always feeling that, had Morgan just kept her mouth shut, the course of life could've been so much different.

He'd been with plenty of women since, but he'd never trusted any of them – including his latest, Tammy, who'd been wooing him with her sarcasm and her body since his first night back in Fayetteville – and he'd never been able to stop hearing Rick's voice: "Loving someone has *got* to mean you trust them, man. Or else what's life about?"

Jesse surely didn't know what life was about these days. Nope, ever since he and Dawn had split and Rick had died – well, the truth was, nothing ever had made much sense, after that.

"Didn't you bring a jacket?" called out a tall woman, holding a rain hat clamped to her head, as Jesse, shivering, descended the ferry's ramp to the tall pier. That had to be Morgan – full of big ideas of what everyone else could do better.

Recognizing her thin nose and the pert angle of her chin, he hitched his guitar up higher on his shoulder and yelled, "Thanks for coming, you're welcome!" Man, that damp wind sure had a bite to it.

She took off her hat and shook out her hair, and he felt a jolt under his skin, an unexpected heat. She'd always been more beautiful than she was likable, but this was ridiculous. She'd actually gotten better with age, long and lean as a fashion model, her brown hair not only longer and more lush than he'd remembered, but glowing with goldish red highlights from the sun.

She looked amazing, glamourous, even in monochrome Army green head-to-toe, from her rain hat and oversized rain jacket all the way down to her skinny jeans and a muddy pair of Wellies.

He walked right up to her, just to prove she couldn't get under his skin. She was only a few inches shorter than him, and he was six foot two. Her fine-boned, make-up-free face was coated in dew from the fog – probably why she looked so out-of-this-world beautiful. She smiled, almost like she was happy to see him. "Same old Jesse," she said. "You must be freezing. And, yes, thanks for coming."

He wanted to make some smartass comment, but he couldn't think. Her face was familiar, but different, too – a little older and wiser, a little more... well, *herself,* was the only thing he could think of. Her mouth curled into a little smile at the corners, and the narrow curves of her upper lip, the thicker contours of the lower, fascinated him.

He caught himself. *Sorry, buddy,* he said to Rick. He was going to have to remember who she was. With the great effort it took to act totally casual, he reached out to nudge her elbow. "Been a long time."

She blinked, maybe even flinched a little. "Come on, let me show you my place," she said. She put on her silly hat and turned and started up the gravel road, toward the village that emerged through the fog on the ghostly hill. Hate seemed far away, and so did the past – at least until Jesse reminded himself of it.

Buddy, if you'd've married someone unattractive, that would've been a whole *lot easier on me,* he told Rick, and followed.

3

"I guess you weren't just whistling Dixie about needing help," Jesse drawled, gazing up at the bare underlayment and scaffolding on Morgan's B&B, framed against the gray sky, his things slung over his shoulder. He made a pleasant picture, she had to admit, though she quickly shut down the thought, reminding herself of what she knew from the past: that of all the people in the world who thought Jesse Stewart was pretty hot, Jesse Stewart was at the top of the list. Even counting all the girls who'd been lining up to be the next in his love-em-and-leave-em cavalcade after he and Dawn broke up. Besides, that dripping-Southern accent of his was just too much. She could hardly believe it was real.

"Come inside," she said. "I'll show you where to put your things."

He dropped his tool bag and belt on the ground and gave her a smile clearly meant to melt any girl's insides. "I'll be getting started right away."

"Great," Morgan said, asking Rick in her head why he'd had to have *this* man as his best friend. A man with a killer grin and bright blue eyes who was just as cocky as all get-out. A cowboy in the worst possible sense of the word.

Well, she wasn't going to let him get to her. He was here for a purpose, and that was that. "I'm going to need it done by the eighth, if you can manage it, okay? That's two weeks from yesterday. I need it done by Columbus Day weekend because the island is so busy then, and people wander in and make reservations for next year – which they won't do if the place looks like a wreck with this scaffolding and all. And then this judge from *Simple Food* is coming on the Tuesday after that, the twelfth."

Jesse looked up at the bare underlayment again, looking slightly dubious, but then he shifted his gaze back to her and gave her that grin again. "Don't worry, I'll be out of your hair by then. Got to get back to work that pays something."

"I told you I'd pay you."

"I told you I wouldn't take it."

She puffed out a breath. "Fine," she said, disproportionately annoyed, hating to think of ending up in his debt. "Come on around back."

He gave his hat brim a little tug. "After you, ma'am."

She sighed again and went ahead, leading him on the stone path that traced the side of the house through the hasta and dogwood. This whole Southern gentleman act was going to get old. "This is our private entrance," she said, leading him into the mudroom at the back of the house. "The guests use the front door." She took off her coat and hung it on one of the hooks that lined the wall.

She felt his eyes on her, and, when she looked, he was watching her like he'd never seen her before. Caught, he shook his head slowly and smiled a little. Her face heated up – a fact she tried to ignore.

"No shoes in the house, please," she said, and sat on the little bench to take off her Wellies. Out of the corner of her eye she saw him set down his things, then suddenly he was sitting beside her, prying off one big cowboy boot. His closeness was a shock, his elbow brushing hers. She tried to concentrate on her own boots, but she could smell on him the fog and mist, plus something earthier that made her notice her own body in a way she hadn't in a very, very long time.

She brushed the feeling aside and assured herself: probably Jesse just reminded her of Rick in some elemental way. They both had that Marine way of moving, the slightly stiff bearing mixed with a terrific ease and strength and comfort in their own skin. Quite a difference from the slouchy lobstermen and tourists she'd been seeing on the island all these years. Yep, that had to be it. Because Jesse Stewart himself was nobody she had any interest in getting closer to. "You aren't planning to wear those to work on my roof, are you?" she said.

"Purely for style," Jesse said, setting his first boot neatly under the bench. "Got my workboots. Now, I'm not much for rules in general, but for you, Mrs. Bailey, I'll do my utmost."

She set down her second Wellie and stood up in her socks like she was unaffected, though her heart was pounding and somehow actually, physically aching, from all these in-your-face reminders of Rick. After Rick was killed, she'd moved from North Carolina as quickly as she could to Maine – where they had no history together; where she had no history at all – so that nothing would remind her of him again, because she'd had all she could do to stop thinking of him every minute as it was. "Nobody calls me Mrs. Bailey anymore," she said. She pointed to his guitar case. "You still play?" She remembered Rick telling her Jesse used to entertain the guys on deployments, that he wrote his own songs and was actually good; that he'd talked about going to Nashville to try to make it, once he got out.

Jesse set his second boot next to the first and stood up. She had to tilt her head back to meet his eyes, which, since she was taller than most people, was unsettling. "They should, and, yeah, I do." His smile showcased the dimple in his cheek. "You? Rick always said you had the voice of an angel."

Morgan winced, remembering all the nights during college and after that she'd spent singing at coffee houses in Wilmington with her band, the three of them dreaming of being the next Cowboy Junkies.

Without Rick to cheer her on, she hadn't had it in her to sing anymore. She'd quit the band, hadn't even kept in touch, and nobody on Seacoast Island knew she'd been a singer at all. She rarely even listened to music, and had gotten used to quiet as the dominant sound in her life. "No," she said, not wanting to think about any of that. "Your shirt's wet. You must be freezing. Come on inside." She turned to lead him into the house.

Her living room had never felt so small as when she faced him again. She hadn't remembered him as so tall, or so overpoweringly good-looking, with that chiseled face, that mussed-up light brown hair poking out from under his hat brim – it had been so short before that she'd never known it was a little curly – and those deep blue eyes that seemed to see straight through to the back of her.

"Nice place," he drawled. Certainly joking: pointing out how small it was, how his head almost reached the ceiling. Morgan's teeth clenched. He might have gotten better looking, but he was the same old smartass as always.

"Here's where you'll sleep," she said. "The couch. Sorry. But the guests don't come in here, so it'll be fairly private. And you get the TV all to yourself."

"What about you?"

She rolled her eyes. "I don't watch much TV. That door over there's my room, and once I'm in for the night, I'm in. You can use the guest bathroom on the second floor. The back stairway there leads almost right to it." She'd thought about letting him share the private bath off her bedroom – something she hadn't considered with the previous roofer – but she'd never dreamed she'd be so oddly drawn to Jesse, at the same time his every little twangy word drove her crazy. *Sorry, sweetheart,* she said to Rick, not sure if she was apologizing for the first or the second part of that. "My guest rooms are all booked for the next couple of weeks, so you can only work on the roof between about ten and five, to keep the noise down."

His eyebrows shot up. "Then I'd best get started." He began unbuttoning his shirt. "Soon as I put on a dry shirt."

Morgan, ridiculously interested in the flash of his skin that showed, pretended not to be. "Want some coffee? Then I can show you where the cedar shakes are. The guy got them ordered and out here, at least."

"Hold everything." Jesse's face clouded over, as he stripped off his shirt, revealing a smooth, muscular chest and giant biceps, one of which had a tattoo snaking around it. Morgan's mouth went dry. "Cedar shakes?" he said. "I thought we were dealing with asphalt, here. No way can I get this house shingled in cedar by myself in thirteen days, working only seven hours a day to boot."

"What do you mean?" She looked at his face, and he looked angry.

"Each one of those babies has to be pounded in *by itself*, Mrs. Bailey. And there're a few tricks which I don't exactly remember from when I helped my dad with his *one-and-only* shake roof back when I was fifteen."

"Everyone around here has them." Why were her *toes* tingling? And her fingers!

"Which is pure crazy, considering you're right on the ocean. You'll be lucky if they last fifteen years, what with all the salt and damp in the air. No, what we're going to have to do is get some asphalt shingles. I can have them on for you lickety-split, last you thirty years."

She folded her arms, making herself focus squarely on the problem. "Absolutely not. This place has to look quaint. It's part of the appeal. Besides, do you know how much those shakes cost me? I can't afford to buy anything else on top of it."

20

"Return them."

"No. The old roof was cedar shakes and this one's going to be, too."

"No way can it be done in the time you're giving me."

"Well, we don't have a choice!" She hadn't gotten this far in the *Simple Food* contest – or had Jesse come all this way – to give up now. "What about if you just do the front? And the sides of the ell that might show. Can you do that in the time we have? Enough to look good in the photograph. I mean, do as much as you possibly can, but start on those sections?"

He sighed. Folded his gigantic arms. "I might could do that."

"Good. Then it's settled." She could breathe again.

"I don't think it's *smart*."

"Your objection is noted. But you came here to help me. Which I *do* appreciate, by the way." She turned to leave, eager to get out of the too-close room, to turn down the charged feeling in her body. "Now, before you start, coffee and scones in the kitchen?"

"Scones?" he said, drawing out the "O" sound to make it ridiculous.

She rolled her eyes again. "Just put on a shirt. House policy: no shirt, no service."

"So I *can't* wear shoes, but I've *got* to wear a shirt. Lotta rules for an old country boy to keep straight around here."

"Just try, Jesse. I have confidence in you." She opened the French doors that led into the B&B's dining room, sneaking a look over her shoulder at him. As long as he was around, showing a little lenience about that shirt policy might not be the *worst* idea.

She shut the door behind her, thinking, *Wait! Jesse Stewart, remember? Old love-em-and-leave-em Jesse?*

Yes, her unusual attraction to him could *only* be because he reminded her of Rick.

She'd just have to get over it. No problem. Spending only a little more time in his obnoxious company ought to do the trick. Starting with coffee and scones in the kitchen. She'd call Lainey and Brick to come over as reinforcements. That would help. She squared her shoulders and went to put on a fresh pot.

"Man, I can't get warm," Jesse said, letting Morgan pour him a third cup of coffee. He'd refused a scone, though she'd offered three times.

"You'll get used to it," Brick said, draping his arm over Lainey's shoulders. "It took some doing, last winter, but I managed. The great thing is the peace and quiet."

"Man, I'm gonna be outta here *long* before winter. Quiet gives me the heebie jeebies. Add cold to it, and I'm a goner."

"The place'll grow on you," Lainey promised, with a little grin in Morgan's direction. Morgan didn't know what *that* was for. Yeah, Jesse was good-looking, but he was also the world's biggest smartass.

Of course, if Lainey was going to try to push Morgan in Jesse's direction, she'd only be doing what Morgan had done to her. Brick had stayed as a guest at Morgan's B&B for a month last summer, and, during that time, Morgan had done her share of subtle matchmaking.

But just because she'd turned out to be right didn't mean that Lainey was going to have any chance to return the favor.

"Grow on me like a fungus, maybe," Jesse said, with a friendly grin.

Everybody laughed except Morgan. "Hey, if you do end up liking it here," Brick said, "I can always use another carpenter. I've got these restoration projects running for the next year, at least, and I'm working on getting funding for a couple more for the year after that. We can get a lot done over the winter, after the tourists leave. Speaking of which, when are you starting up your yoga class again, Morgan?"

"Brick," Lainey scolded, "she has enough on her plate."

Morgan usually loved teaching her weekly yoga class down at the Village Hall, but, this summer, with preparing for this contest, something had had to give.

"I know, but I'm getting out of shape," Brick said. "So's everybody else on the island."

"Me, too," Morgan said. "Things have been so crazy, I haven't even been practicing myself."

"You look in shape to me," Jesse said, looking her up and down.

Her face heated up, and Lainey grinned. Morgan decided the best course of action was to ignore both her and Jesse. "I'll get yoga going again after this judge has come and gone, Brick," Morgan promised. "And don't be trying to recruit Jesse. He's only going to be here a couple of weeks. Then he's got a whole life in North Carolina to get back to."

"Well, a *dog*, anyway," Jesse said. "My dad's watching Buster for me. Buster came back from Afghanistan with me."

"Aw, Buster! What a cute name," Lainey said. "We have a golden. Ella. She's still appealing to our cat, Henry James, to be friends. It might take a lifetime for him to agree, but at least he's letting her sleep in the bedroom with the rest of us."

"That's sweet," Jesse said. "You two have any kids?"

"Oh, no," Lainey said. "We've only been married three months." But she gave Brick a look that made Morgan wonder. Was there a chance...? Morgan was both jealous and happy to think of her best friend becoming a mom; it was a chance she never expected to have herself. She'd have to ask Lainey about it later, in private.

"Jesse," Morgan said, "if you won't eat a scone, will you let me make you something else? What would you like?"

He brightened. "You know, I *would* really like me a grilled cheese. It isn't too early for lunch, is it?"

"That'll be fine. Lainey and Brick, you want some?"

"I'd better get back to the shop," Lainey said. "I left Hannah in charge, but, with it being Saturday, it might get busy. Besides, she doesn't know about the books like I do. Not that I know about wine like she does!" After a tree fell on Lainey's shop last summer in a storm, a wealthy summer family named the Champlains had offered to become her silent partners in rebuilding and expanding, because Lainey had helped stop some land that their family had designated as a preserve from being developed illegally. The Champlains' daughter, Hannah, who'd been working in retail in New York, had been hired as Lainey's assistant manager and sommelier. Hannah also made jewelry, which she called "Silver Star Designs" and marketed on etsy.

"I should get back, too," Brick said. "Got to check in with my guys on one of the projects."

Jesse said to Brick, "Morgan's having me use cedar shake shingles. You do much with these? 'Cause I have *not.*"

Brick shrugged. "I can take a look. Probably lots of advice on YouTube, too."

"Right! Hadn't thought of that. Been in the giant sandbox too long, I guess."

"Great," Morgan said. "I'll make you your lunch, Jesse, and, when you're ready, just come in."

"Cool," he said, and Brick waved goodbye to Morgan and followed him out.

"What a cutie," Lainey said, under her breath.

"Ha," Morgan said. "A wolf in sheep's clothing is what he is. Hey, is there something going on with you? I saw the way you looked at Brick when Jesse asked you about kids."

Lainey laughed. "I'll tell you later. I mean, if there's anything to tell! See you tomorrow morning for the tasting group, right? I can't wait to see what you've come up with this time." She grinned and was gone.

Wondering over just how huge the change to island life would be if Lainey *was* pregnant, Morgan made Jesse a grilled sandwich of *chevre*, roasted beets, and baby arugula, with sweet potato fries on the side. When he came in, his eyebrows shot up at the sight of it laid out beautifully on one of her blue plates. "Too fancy for me," he declared, then polished off the sandwich in four bites. "I was thinking cheddar," he said, in review.

"I'll be better next time," she said dryly, then showed him to her desk so he could watch YouTube how-tos. She went to service the guest rooms, and, all afternoon, every time she came through to put in another load of laundry in the little room off the kitchen, he was saying something at the screen: "Oh, hell, no," or, "You wouldn't know your ass from a hole in the ground, there, buddy." He finally got out on the roof about four o'clock, and she went outside once to hear him cursing as he struggled with the first row of shingles. Her prospects for getting the roof done in time were *not* looking good.

Hoping to encourage him, she made a nice dinner of poached salmon with dill and baby asparagus. Usually, she didn't bother much with dinner for herself – or lunch, come to think of it. She never really felt that hungry, probably because she was always eating a bite of this or that while working in the garden or cooking breakfast. Her preparations for the meal she prepared for her guests could take place at any hour of the day, and often did.

She'd tried to make her life a little easier last spring by upgrading from a wood cookstove to a gas range, but then she'd started making far more complicated dishes, so she ended up getting up just as early as she had when she'd had to start a fire. Probably, truth be told, she was spending even more time on breakfasts than she ever used to. Especially since she'd been trying to come up with recipes for the contest.

Jesse took off his hat for dinner, and the way his hair curled a little over his ears gave her an odd, trembly feeling in her knees. It faded, fortunately, when he launched into a long soliloquy on how he didn't know what was "with" all these "baby" vegetables, and how he knew a thing or two about that very marketing ploy, because, as a kid, he'd pulled all the carrots that had failed to thrive in his parents' garden, packaged them up "real nice in those fancy looking plastic clamshell things, you know, and tied 'em with pretty bows and all" and sold each box for three times the price of a bunch of regular carrots. "I mean, they were just *little*, that was all. Failures. They were about to go in the compost otherwise, or my dad might've fed 'em to the pigs."

He didn't offer to help with the dishes, instead watching another couple of YouTube how-tos, then disappearing into the private part of the house. After she'd finished cleaning up and doing what she could for tomorrow's breakfast, she knocked lightly on the French doors, feeling strangely nervous. In fact, if she hadn't *had* to pass through where he was to get to her room – at least without going outside, where she chanced encountering the skunk she'd seen in the garden last week – she'd have avoided him for sure.

"Come in!" he yelled, and he was sitting on the couch, the TV on. He was shirtless again, of course, and he'd cranked the heat way up. The lamp light glowed on his skin, and he grinned at her like he was about to announce her phone number at the annual meeting of Shirtless Cowboys United.

Annoyingly, her body got all tingly again at the sight of him. She tried to ignore it. She hadn't been in close quarters with a man in a long time, that was all.

"Want to watch TV?" he said.

Like she was going to plop herself down on the couch next to him! She shook her head, trying not to blush – or stare. "Got to get up early. Have everything you need?"

"Think so."

"Great. Well, good night," she said, heading for her room, and, before she shut her door, she heard him say, "Sleep tight," and even *that* sounded like a smartass comment, coming from him.

She got into her pajamas, conscious of him on the other side of the door, wishing these two weeks would just be over. *Sorry, sweetheart,* she told Rick, *but I wish it could be anybody else, here helping me.* She crawled in under her covers and flopped over, trying to get comfortable – impossible, when her body felt charged up again. How could Jesse, of all people, be getting under her skin like this?

Suddenly – she couldn't believe it – she heard *music* coming from the other room. A guitar. One loud chord, then another, then Jesse cursing. A pause, then the first chord again. He wasn't even trying to be quiet. "The highway stretches out," he sang in a pure, clear tone. Great. Jesse really *was* a singing cowboy.

She groaned, yanked her pillow over her head.

He was back on the first chord again. "The highway stretches long," he sang, then stopped again.

She tossed off the covers, grabbed a fleece to throw on over her pajamas, and stormed out. "Jesse!"

He looked at her innocently, set down the pencil he'd just jotted a note with, and strummed a fresh chord. "Yes?" He pronounced the word with two syllables.

"I have six people upstairs trying to sleep or at least have a quiet moment. Not to mention me, who's got to get up at five to start breakfast."

He stopped playing. "Are you joking? You're going to tell me I can't play? I always write at night. To unwind. Helps me sleep."

"Please," Morgan said. "Have some consideration for the other people under this roof. You'll only be here two weeks." At this moment, that sounded *way* too long.

He put down his guitar, looking like he felt the same. "Another *rule*," he said. Then he looked her up and down. "Nice p-jays."

"At least I'm wearing *something*," she said, as her face heated up. She'd long ago stopped thinking about what she wore to bed, and these flannel pajamas were meant for comfort, not for looks. She'd never had cause to be embarrassed about that before. "Good night." She wheeled and went back into her room, pulling the door shut firmly behind her.

She got into bed, hearing him out there putting his guitar back into his case.

I'm sorry, sweetheart, she said again, because she'd wished, when Jesse saw her, that she'd been wearing something more presentable. Slightly sexy, even.

Just so he wouldn't think she was a loser – that was all. Right?

She didn't know how she was ever going to get to sleep.

4

In the morning, Jesse woke up later than he'd meant to – not that it mattered, since he wasn't supposed to start working till *ten*, for God's sake – and got annoyed all over again when he recalled Morgan shushing him and his guitar last night. He blamed her for the fact he'd tossed and turned for hours till he'd finally fallen into some crazy dream-filled version of sleep.

These two weeks were going to be even worse than he'd thought. He hadn't realized he'd have to tippy-toe around all the time out of "consideration" for Morgan's guests. Not that they were showing any for *him* this morning. He could hear them on the other side of those French doors, laughing, their silverware clinking on plates as they ate what was certainly some kind of ridiculous frou-frou breakfast.

Though, whatever it was, it smelled pretty darn good.

Still, beautiful as Morgan was, between her unreasonable expectations, her hoity-toity ways, and all her rules, he couldn't help but wonder how his buddy had handled being married to her.

Of course, Rick had been deployed over half the time he'd been with her. Maybe that explained how they'd managed to get along – and also why, from what Jesse had heard from Rick's parents, Morgan hadn't reached out since the funeral or taken them up on their invitations to visit or spend the holidays. After a couple years, they'd pretty much given up on her, which had broken their hearts all over again.

The way Jesse figured, Morgan just must not have loved Rick that much; the relationship of three-plus years clearly just hadn't cut that deep in her. Look at the flip way, yesterday, she'd said, "Nobody calls me Mrs. Bailey anymore," like Rick was ancient history she couldn't be bothered with. Yep, the way Jesse saw it, where in most people beat a heart, in Morgan Bailey sat a cool hunk of iceberg lettuce, wilting.

She must have just had Rick fooled into thinking otherwise, while he was alive. And now here Jesse was, suffering the consequences of that fooling all these years later, having promised to look after a woman who if, had he lived, Rick might not even still be married to, what with how faithless she obviously was. Never mind that Rick had believed they were soulmates and shared a perfect love. In Jesse's book, Morgan's behavior just went to show there was no such thing.

"There he is!" Morgan said from where she stood behind the island in the kitchen. "Glad you could put in an appearance!" Jesse'd gone around outside the house and back in the front door, trying to avoid making some grand entrance through the French doors directly into where the guests were eating, only to find that not only were six people eating around the dining room table, but a whole crowd – all men except for two – was standing around the island with Morgan. They each had a pile of small plates in front of them, forks in their hands, and happy looks on their faces. Jesse recognized Lainey and Brick, who both smiled their greetings.

"Everyone, meet Jesse!" Morgan said. She was wearing the same thing she had yesterday – a white shirt with olive green skinny jeans; no makeup – and looked as gorgeous as most women would have only if they'd spent hours fixing themselves up. "My late husband's friend who's here to do my roof." There was a chorus of hellos.

"What's all this?" Jesse said.

"My tasting group! These folks – except Lainey and Brick, of course – these folks all work as chefs at the restaurants and hotels, and they're helping me fine-tune my recipes for the contest. Meet Brad, Ralph, Kevin, Paul, Uriah, Tom, and Sam."

"Samantha, if that helps," said a woman with short, dark hair with long purple bangs that swept across her forehead. Everyone laughed.

"And over there," Morgan went on, pointing to the group around the dining room table, "our guests. Misty and Paul from Connecticut, Yolanda and George from New York, and Gracie and Bill from Bangor." They all waved.

"Oh, the poor man hasn't even had his coffee yet," one of the chefs crooned, and one of the men at the table said, "*We're* all leaving today, so there won't be a quiz."

"Great. All right, then," Jesse said, amazed – yet not – that Morgan had assembled such a crowd just to admire her cooking. Of all the arrogant and foolish things. "I'll just get my coffee and I'll be outta your hair." Morgan turned and reached to get him a mug from the cupboard. Jesse said, "Brick, buddy, any chance you got any free time today to work on a roof?"

"I can try to get over this afternoon," Brick said. He smiled at Morgan. "If Morgan needs help, we all want to help her."

So why the hell, Jesse wondered, had he had to drive up all the way from North Carolina?

"Aren't you going to try the Polynesian French toast?" said another of the chefs, a forty-something guy with a graying-blond beard. "The braised pineapple-banana filling and the blueberry lemon verbena compote'll knock your socks right off."

"Of course, you missed the blackberry waffle bread pudding with citrus crème anglaise last week," said a young guy with spiky red hair. "That might've even beat out this one." A round of objections from the chefs, though a roly-poly guy with buzz-cut blond hair and a friendly, flushed face voiced agreement.

Jesse held up a hand. "*Entirely* too many syllables to eat for breakfast, you ask me. I like one syllable, maybe two. Eggs. Pan-cakes. Cof-fee." Everyone laughed again.

"Yes, Jesse's got a real refined palate," Morgan said.

He did not appreciate her sarcasm one bit. "Mind if I get to work, long as I don't start pounding till after you all are done? I've got some things to lay out and such."

"Of course," Morgan said, handing him a steaming mug. "Thanks. You sure you don't want anything to eat?"

She seemed a bit distressed over the idea. Probably she just wanted another person to compliment her.

"Sure as can be." He raised his mug to the crowd. "Y'all be careful," he said, and made his exit out the front, sipping coffee as their chatter resumed behind him. A tasting group, for God's sake. A group assembled for the pure and elegant purpose of bowing before her, was more like it.

Man, she did make good coffee, though.

"Hey, Jesse, come down here!" he heard Morgan call, much later, as he was up on the roof cursing to himself, struggling to place a shim under a shingle, nail between his lips, hammer in his hand – the videos he'd watched and most everything he'd read had advocated for pounding the roof into place the old-fashioned way, no nail gun involved. He'd heard Morgan's guests file out, then all had gone quiet except for his pounding. He'd managed to get about a two-by-two square done. He hoped Brick would show up later, and would know what he was doing, because Jesse had little prayer of getting this whole project done all by himself in Morgan's timeframe.

He took the nail out from between his lips. "What?" He couldn't see her from where he was.

"Come down here!"

He set down his hammer and everything else and backed over to the scaffolding. "Hold the scaffolding, why don't you?" he said, and she did, and he got on it and made his way down, brushing against her inadvertently when he got to the last two steps, feeling that strange charge under his skin again.

Well, nobody'd ever accused him of being immune to a beautiful woman. In fact, his flirting instincts had already kicked in a couple of times with Morgan. He was going to have to be careful to keep those in check.

She'd tied up her hair, and, when she smiled, he liked the way her pretty green eyes crinkled at their corners. She reached down to pick up a little basket and a travel mug, holding them out to him. "Fresh coffee and muffins. You didn't have any breakfast, so I thought you might be hungry."

He eyed them suspiciously. "Are they Polynesian French muffins?"

She laughed. "No. Just regular old blueberry muffins."

He surrendered, suddenly realizing he was starving. "All right. Thanks. I am a little hungry." He grabbed a muffin – it was warm, maybe just out of the oven – and took the coffee. He sat down on the front stoop. "Take a load off," he invited her, though he still wasn't sure what to make of her gesture. It wasn't like she'd been acting exactly happy he was there.

"I've got to clean rooms."

"Five minutes won't kill you."

"Okay," she said, sounding a bit suspicious of *him.* "Let me get my coffee." She went past him up the steps and inside. He polished off the muffin in three bites and grabbed another. The day was sunny, not too cold. Boats were moving in the harbor. The ferry was at the dock.

This island was a strange place to him, what with all the rock and water. He was a guy who loved the lush earth where he came from; who loved knowing that, if you planted a seed, it would grow. But something about this place *was* inching up on him a little. Even if it was ridiculously cold for late September.

Morgan came back out and sat down on the other side of the same step. She sipped her coffee. It was kind of nice, actually, sitting there peaceably with her, almost like they were friends. He'd never had a woman friend before.

Her voice broke the silence. "So, how's everything been going?"

As he finished his second muffin, the taste went slightly sour. "Now, I can't have you coming out every three hours with a gol-darn *snack* asking me for a progress report, or I'm never going to get anywhere."

She rolled her eyes. "I meant 'in your life,' Sherlock. How's everything been going in your life? It's called making conversation. And I wouldn't *have* to interrupt your work if you'd eat a proper breakfast so I wouldn't have to worry about you falling off the roof or some stupid thing because your blood sugar's low. And, believe me, I would prefer not to have to interrupt you."

"Oh." Jesse felt like a fool at that, but, for some reason, he didn't much mind. Maybe being friends might actually be possible. "All right. Well, thanks for asking. Everything's been all right. Got out a couple months ago and went to help out my dad. He's counting on me to take over the business when he retires."

"Hmm," she said. "Don't you have your own dreams?"

As always, thinking she knew best. "The old man's been on his own since my mom left, basically," Jesse said. "My older brother's a goldarn *banker*, so he's no help.

My dad claims to need me. Anyway, he says that the company and his farm is the legacy he wants to leave me, and that's it's my job to work to claim it. His words." Jesse wasn't sure he bought all that, but it did *sound* good. Mostly.

"Hmm," she said again. "Well, you must *have* dreams. What about Nashville?"

"Who doesn't?" But his were buried down deep these days, and nothing he wanted to talk about – especially not his old fool notion of going to Nashville. "What about you? How's everything been going for you?"

She pointed back over her shoulder at the B&B. "Pretty much what you see here."

That seemed, suddenly, a little sad. Empty. "I see you work awful hard. Got a man in your life? I mean, I know there's no one 'Facebook official,' as the saying goes, but maybe you're just keeping your private life private. Seems to me you could use a little help with this place."

"No. No one since Rick."

His eyebrows went up. "No one?" He couldn't have been more surprised if she'd said she was in love with Big Bird.

She shrugged, smiled a little, ruefully. "A hard act to follow."

He could practically feel the files in his brain being reshuffled. "Well," was all he could say at first, and then he blurted, "But you're knockdown gorgeous!"

Her cheeks got pink. "Stop. I'm not." She twisted the plain gold band he hadn't noticed before around her finger. She was still wearing her wedding ring? After six years?

He was too astonished to think what to say about that, so he stumbled on. "You might be trying to play it down, wearing that type of clothes and such, but I'm serious. Man, you ever wear *actual* clothes, or, like, a red dress or something, you'd have men on that ferry boat all day long coming out here to try to win you."

She laughed. "A good reason not to start. Anyway, I don't like to put time into thinking about what to wear. This way I can just go to Bean's once a winter and stock up on green jeans and white shirts. Easy."

He was mystified. She wore the same outfit *every* day? "You could always shop online. I mean, so I hear. I recall you used to like to dress pretty."

"I only got high-speed internet this spring, and I haven't exactly had time for shopping. Anyway, at this point, if people on this island saw me in anything but this, they'd say, 'Who are you and what have you done with Morgan?'"

"Surely that isn't so."

She shrugged, twisted her wedding ring once more, then looked up. "What about you? Hasn't anyone tried to make an honest man out of you since Dawn?"

He wasn't ready to change the subject, but maybe he'd have to work on her again later. "Plenty have tried," he drawled. "None quite took. Speaking of Dawn, me and you have never discussed how you were the cause of the ruin of that whole thing. Thanks for that."

Morgan laughed shortly. "I didn't cause it. *She* caused it. She was stepping out on you."

"Yeah, whatever." Now he wished he hadn't brought it up. He and Morgan had actually been having a pleasant time.

"What do you mean, 'whatever'?" Morgan said. "She *was*. Rick said she even admitted it to you. Didn't she?"

"There were other things to consider."

"*What* other things? She was cheating on you!"

He was aggravated now. This was that same old black-and-white view she'd always had. "Morgan, listen. What you don't understand about life is that, for most of us mere mortals, disappointment's just a part of life. Anyone I'm with is bound to disappoint me, some way. Take Tammy from back home. Dating her two months now, right? She's been texting me nonstop the whole three days I've been gone, knowing I don't text and hate to text and won't text, like I've told her. I've called her from your phone, since you said you didn't mind me using it. But does she answer? No. Or even once return a call, when I've told her to call your landline number? No. She goddamn texts me again. But I figure, whatever. That's her thing. She's twenty-three goddamn years old."

"Twenty-three? Oh, what a good idea, Jesse," Morgan said, and she wasn't smiling. She let down her hair and shook it out, and it was wavy from the dampness in the air. Just like yesterday at the dock, seeing it made his skin heat up, his heart stop a little. "And it sounds to me like she's being disrespectful to you and your wishes," she went on, oblivious.

Jesse shook his head and took a swallow of coffee, feeling a little stupid, trying to collect himself. "My point is, whatever. You know? Ever since my mom got a notion she'd canned enough tomatoes in her life and left my dad when I was fourteen, just so she could get her college degree and go work in some office in Raleigh, I've seen it clear as day. Nobody can be like you and Rick were forever. Thinking each other hung the moon. You know, that probably wasn't even true. You were hardly together at all, in truth, and, if he'd've made it home, you'd have sooner or later seen each other more clear." He was getting revved up now, and barely noticed the frown on Morgan's face. "You'd have seen each of you was just a disappointing human being, just like every other disappointing human being on earth. And for you to sit here and say you're spending your life alone because nobody can measure up to him, well, that's just being a plain fool. That's just not seeing *reality*."

She laughed bitterly. "Reality, Jesse? You don't know *anything* about me and Rick. And if reality's where you live, I don't want to go there. You're just making excuses and saying everybody's disappointing because that's what *you* are."

"Aw, Morgan, listen, I'm sorry," he said, wishing he could take it all back. He never did know when to quit, at least according to what his mom said. And the last thing he should've done was to insult Morgan and Rick's love, when she'd just told him she was still carrying a big fat torch for him. When he'd just seen that she still wore her ring.

Seemed like when she'd let down her hair his brain had lost its bearings – not that that was any real excuse, or anything he could tell her. "I really am."

But Morgan wasn't hearing him. "Dawn wasn't the problem, was she? You were. Because you're a cowboy. In the worst sense of the word. Bound to desert anybody who ever tries to love you. And you *know* it." Now *she* was revved up. "That's right. You were so sure you were going to disappoint her that you couldn't stand it. So you pushed her away and made it into her fault. Which is probably the same thing you've done with every girl since, all the ones who didn't 'take.' *You're* the disappointing human being, Jesse. No wonder you wear that hat. It's like you're warning everybody to stay away, and, if they don't pay attention, that's their fault."

He laughed, hurt. "Well, now, why don't you tell me how you really feel?"

Morgan tossed her hair again. "I just feel sorry for you, carrying that hopeless outlook around with you everywhere you go."

Jesse's heart felt pinched. "And I feel sorry for *you*, weighed down under that big old *chip* on your shoulder. Yeah, you lost your husband when you were way too young. Yeah, it ain't fair."

She winced. "What a big heart you have."

"I lost my best friend over there. And got my engagement broken up. A heart gets tired."

She stood, looking upset. "I'm sorry," she snapped. "But that isn't the same as losing your husband." She turned and went inside, banging the door behind her.

He slammed the travel mug to the grass, stood and started up the scaffolding. *Friends! Right. The sooner I get out of here, the better,* he thought.

41

Me and my big goddamn mouth, he thought.

Morgan slammed the door and ran straight upstairs, ready to strip some beds and beat some pillows into sub-mission – anything that would get her anger out. Wow, what a mistake, going out to sit down with Jesse! Even baking him those muffins had probably been a mis-take, born of her ridiculous need to make sure every-one around her was well-fed. But then, thinking – even for a moment – that she should try to be friends with him! They'd never liked each other when Rick was alive. What had made her think they could get along now? Just because he was here and she was stuck with him!

She didn't want to think how much of her effort might have been because she found him so undeniably physically attractive. She'd seen him sleeping at five this morning when she'd walked through the living room on her way to the kitchen. He'd been sprawled on the couch, his feet hanging over one end, a blanket cover-ing only as much as a pair of shorts would. His perfectly toned, pleasantly large bare legs and feet, chest and arms had made a very enticing picture. And his face – peaceful and handsome and vulnerable in sleep; almost sweet, in a way that never showed when he was awake – had fooled her, she guessed.

Surely that was why, a few minutes ago, when he'd said he was dating a girl back home, she'd felt a small wave of disappointment roll through. And why, when he'd charitably called her "knockdown gorgeous," not just her face but her whole body had heated up.

It couldn't be that what Lainey had told her this morning had gotten into Morgan's head, could it? After Jesse'd made his appearance at the tasting group, Lainey had pulled her aside, grinning, and said, "There's some pretty evident chemistry between you two. Like, *firecrackers across the room* chemistry. Why didn't you tell me?"

"Oh, no," Morgan had said. "You're imagining things."

But maybe she'd started to wonder: if someone else could see it, did that mean it was there?

No more of that, she told herself now. *No more wondering, no more musing, no more looking at him when he sleeps.*

To think he could still blame her for what happened with Dawn! And then, even worse, that he'd say such things about her and Rick. That what they'd had hadn't been true!

She would be civil to him, and that was all. *I don't care how good he looks, or how long I've been alone, or how it might seem that getting closer to him might bring me back closer to Rick* – that *is the thing that isn't true!*

She got busy stripping a bed, and she was talking to Rick again – *I'm sorry, sweetheart, so, so sorry* – and suddenly tears were in her throat – *but sometimes you seem so far away.*

5

"Polynesian French toast with braised pineapple-banana filling?" said the man standing in Morgan's front room. "Oh, yes, we had that this morning up at Woods and Water."

Morgan couldn't believe what she was hearing. The man's wife, beside him, blinked big brown eyes behind her glasses. "Yes, the blueberry lemon verbena compote was amazing!"

The pair had stopped in at Morgan's to, as the man put it, "check out the competition, see if we might want to stay here next year instead," and Morgan had been telling them about her breakfasts. Her major selling point, and, as far as she was concerned, still working to beat out the competition. After all, shared bathroom or not, *she'd* been booked up for this weekend when this couple sought a reservation a month ago; Woods and Water had had openings. (They did have two more guest rooms than she did, but still.)

But now this news dropped on her like a bomb.

She tried to keep her cool. "Blackberry waffle bread pudding with citrus crème anglaise?"

"Had that yesterday!" said the woman, with a triumphant smile.

"Boy, that was *good*," the man said. "So you're telling me you copy their breakfasts here? What, are you franchised or something?" He laughed at his own joke.

"No!" Morgan objected, only to be interrupted by a pounding on the roof – Jesse, hammering in a shingle. The noise had been constant all week. Morgan's every nerve was aggravated. And the headache she'd had since Wednesday was only getting worse, with this news.

"And you have *construction* going on," said the man. "We saw the scaffolding."

"Very temporary!" Morgan said. "It'll be done in about a week." She prayed. Though Jesse wasn't exactly making lightning progress. Today was Saturday already – only six days from the deadline she'd set for him – and he was nearly finished with the front of the main section of the house, but the two sides of the ell that would show in photographs remained untouched. Brick had been helping when he could, but that wasn't much.

More pounding. The couple looked at Morgan with concern. The woman rested a hand on her husband's arm. "Well, dear, it *is* nice and quiet up there in the woods. I know we wanted a view, but the private bathrooms… the same breakfasts…"

The man shrugged and gave Morgan an apologetic smile. "Guess it's settled, then. Good luck to you."

Watching them turn and walk out, Morgan wanted to scream. Woods and Water was serving *her* creations for their breakfasts! Her signature creations that she was planning to use in ten days to wow the *Simple Food* judge into awarding her $10,000 as the national grand champion of bed-and-breakfast breakfasts! The $10,000 that was going to help her keep pace with the competition!

No way would she win any prize if the judge learned that the very same breakfasts were being served by that competition up the hill.

And, if Woods and Water was serving great breakfasts along with offering amenities like private bathrooms, they could, in the long run, very well steal most of Morgan's clientele.

With a shaking hand, she dialed Lainey's number. Lainey was aghast at the news. "But how are they *getting* the recipes?"

"Clearly, one of our tasting group is a mole. They must be figuring out the recipes from taste and sharing them. God, why did I ask them to help? I don't even know them. And now one of them is sabotaging me."

"Who would do such a thing? And why? What could any of them have to gain?"

"I don't know. I don't think I have any enemies!"

Lainey sighed. "But even *with* the recipes, I heard the DuPages can hardly scramble an egg without ruining it. Or, Mrs. DuPage, anyway, since Mr. DuPage is hardly involved."

"Right. Whoever it is must be cooking for them, too." Morgan felt grim.

"But why wouldn't we have heard about that, if they'd hired someone? Oh, shoot, Morg, I've got a customer. I'll call you back."

"Okay." Morgan hung up, opened the computer, and got Woods and Water's bedandbreakfast.com entry up on the screen. Hate seeped through her when she saw it.

Sure enough, reviews from earlier in the season panned their breakfasts, but, in the last two weeks, they'd gotten four raves. *Don't know what the people who complained about breakfast are talking about,* one said. *We had amazing Georgia peach and mascarpone-stuffed crepes with praline sauce that made us scrape our plates and ask for more!*

Another of Morgan's recipes. And, for God's sake, they had her blackberry waffle bread pudding listed as their "Signature Dish"!

"You look like you seen a ghost," came a voice – Jesse's. She'd been so wrapped up in what she was reading that she hadn't realized the pounding on the roof had stopped.

All week, since their fight on Sunday, they'd been keeping their distance, being civil but nothing more. She'd fix him a plate for each meal and he'd eat in front of the TV. It was fine by her, not to have to listen to his critiques of her cooking, though she'd toned down what she gave him by several notches. BLTs were his favorite – "I never get tired of these!" he raved – so she'd been making him two every day for lunch on sourdough, adding chipotle-dill mayo to give them a kick. (She actually liked them, too; one day, she even made one for herself and ate it on the sly.) The weather had been cold enough that his shirt had stayed on, which helped Morgan keep her promise to herself not to be checking him out every time she saw him. And she'd been wearing her old flannel pajamas – and her usual greens and whites – without apology even to herself. A few nights, she'd seen him walk out of the house with his guitar case slung over his shoulder. She assumed he was going to find a quiet place to play, and she hadn't asked where it was.

But right now she was so upset she couldn't keep her feelings inside. "This... This!" she sputtered.

"Spit it out," he teased.

Could he actually just not help himself from being a complete smartass *all the time*? And why did have to look so good, anyway – even just standing there in a flannel shirt and jeans, his leather tool belt around his waist, hammer hanging down against his hip? She'd been disciplined about not looking toward the couch when she passed by in the early mornings, but what was she supposed to do when he showed up in front of her, looking the way he did?

She caught herself, looking back at the screen. "Woods and Water is serving my breakfasts. The ones I was going to make for the judge." She was overcome with sudden disbelief, near despair. She'd been preparing for this contest since June. She'd made the arrangements to have the roof fixed. She'd tried two dozen different breakfast ideas, chosen the three she'd make, then tested and re-tested them to the point where they barely needed tweaking. She'd been so focused that, according to Brick, anyway, the whole island's health was suffering on account of her canceling her yoga classes! Now here she was, ten days from the judge's arrival, and the roof wasn't done and she had nothing to cook that would seem the least bit original.

And, with Woods and Water serving her breakfasts on a daily basis, now, instead of being on the cusp of unparalleled publicity and a big expansion, she was in danger of losing everything.

"Weird," Jesse said. "Well, can't you just make something else?"

She glared at him. "Nothing that would be perfect enough to win. Do you have any idea how much work went into creating those recipes? Now they're serving them up there at the goddamn Holiday Inn Express and my customers are going to defect in favor of the private bathrooms!"

His eyes narrowed as he took that in, then he said, "Listen, I know you don't want more bad news right this minute, but the wind's kicking up pretty good. Looks like a good rain coming. I need you to come out and help me tarp in case it downpours. We've got some potential leak situations, I'm afraid."

Morgan jumped up and followed him.

As she climbed the scaffolding to the roof, the wind was whipping, and she kept having to stop to brush her hair out of her eyes. She was conscious of Jesse below. He'd insisted on holding the scaffolding while she climbed, though he climbed it by himself all the time and probably weighed twice what she did. "Don't be looking at my butt," she called down.

"I'm trying to make sure you don't fall. You're welcome."

She made it the last couple steps and clambered onto the platform. The view of the harbor was spectacular, and the ominous clouds on the horizon seemed a fitting omen, a sign that her world was indeed about to come crashing down. "Hurry up, Jesse!"

She heard the soft clang of metal, step after slow step, the scaffolding wobbling slightly as Jesse climbed, then she heard his voice, coming closer. "Hey, how'd those folks get a hold of your recipes, anyway?"

Why wasn't he more worried about the roof? "I think there's a mole in the tasting group."

His head rose above the scaffolding, and angry blue eyes met hers. "Are you serious?" He didn't wear his hat while he was working, and his hair ruffled in the wind. "One of them twerp chefs?"

Despite everything, she laughed. "Yes."

He shook his head. "Goddamn." He set a blue tarp on the platform and climbed up beside her.

Wow, the platform was not very big! His sudden closeness made her more nervous than being up high did, and she burst out talking. "The thing is, I *know* they can't cook, so even with good recipes, how are they doing it? I mean, probably they've hired someone in secret, because I can't imagine I wouldn't have heard if they'd hired someone openly. But to have to read about this on the internet! That's what happens when everybody gets busy with summer visitors. Nobody gets together and gossips."

"God forbid." Jesse started opening the tarp. The wind caught it and it ballooned. Jesse cursed. Morgan grabbed the flapping end. "Good!" he said, spreading it against the roof. "Now, hold on there. Be careful."

He was being so sweet, and he looked so very good. *Stop. Keep talking.* "But, I mean, everybody knew how important this contest was to me and that I've been busting my tail to really push the envelope on what I can reasonably create for a breakfast, right? What are we doing?" Her hair was whipping around again.

"Getting this peak covered." He took the hammer from his tool belt and pounded in a few quick nails. Wow, she'd never realized how much she liked the sight of a man with a hammer. "You go on up and secure that end," he said. She climbed onto the roof, and he passed her an extra hammer. She teetered slightly, grabbing it. "Be careful," he said, climbing up the little chicken ladder on the roof itself. "There's a box of nails over there. I'm gonna bring this end on over and get it nailed down."

"*You* be careful," she said, watching him.

"What do you think I've *been* doing?"

Rain started, a few fat drops. Jesse cursed again and crawled faster.

"Take your time," Morgan said, reaching for the box of nails, struggling to keep one knee on the tarp to keep it from blowing up.

"You won't be saying that when you end up with your attic dripping water down onto your guest rooms."

True enough. Just when you thought things couldn't get worse, they always could. She concentrated on pounding in nails along the edge of the roof. As she worked her way toward the peak, she felt him tugging on his side, then heard him pounding, too. The rain was falling harder, and she was getting soaked. She'd run out of the house without stopping for a jacket or her Wellies – she was wearing the ballet flats she usually only wore indoors – and the wind and rain seemed to be growing colder. But there was no time to climb back down and get something to keep her dry, so she just kept going.

She was pounding nails along the side of the back, unfinished part of the roof, where there weren't even any boards nailed to walk on, when she saw out of the corner of her eye Jesse crawling around to secure the fourth side of the tarp, and then he was pounding nails again. Just as she was finishing her side, he was coming up on her, finishing, too. She turned, and he was right there. He grinned. "You poor wet cat."

She was freezing, but she couldn't help laughing. "*You're* a poor wet cat! What about the ell? Do we need to tarp that?"

Jesse looked up at the sky, squinting, making the point that it was pouring. "I don't think at this point we *can*. Wouldn't be safe."

"Maybe we could spread a tarp inside the attic."

His blue eyes were intense, even in the gray light and through the falling rain. "Good idea. First, we've got to get down." He looked up the blue slope of the tarped roof. Rivulets of water were forming and running down as the rain fell. "Hell. We can't climb up that thing. Guess I did not plan this particularly well. How about you wait here? I'll go around, get down, and bring you a ladder. You got an extra one?"

"In the garden shed, yes. But I can go around, too."

"Do not be silly," he said, and set off inching his way around. His shirt was wet and showed off the shape of his muscles as he moved.

She looked away. If he kept being so nice, she was going to have a real problem. *Sorry, sweetheart,* she told Rick. "Sitting here helpless is not exactly my cup of tea," she said to Jesse.

"Poor baby," he said.

6

When Jesse finally reached the ground, making his way carefully down the slick scaffolding, he let out a breath of relief. The minutes he'd spent crawling around the roof had felt like a lifetime, and Morgan must be suffering mightily, sitting in the cold rain. Quick as he could, he grabbed the ladder from the garden shed and brought it to where she was, letting it fall against the gutter near her feet, which got her attention. "Finally!" she said, peering down at him, but then she smiled, and she looked radiant, soaked though she was.

He held the sides of the ladder. "Slow and steady wins the race," he called up to her. "After all this, do not fall on my head. Mind, the ladder's slippery."

"Ha ha. I wouldn't think of it." She turned and got herself onto the ladder, and he looked up as she descended, letting the rain fall in his face. Same as when he'd watched her climb up the scaffolding, he did not mind the view of the back of those green jeans one bit. As she came closer, he tried to look away, but then indulged in a look back – just in time to see her foot slip. His heart lurched. Without thinking, he snatched her by the waist and lifted her down.

"Whoa!" She whirled to face him, looking flabbergasted. Her shirt was soaked through, and her hair was in wet ropes. Rain fell between them and all around.

"Sorry! I didn't want you to fall." It was all he could do to keep from grabbing her waist again and pulling her near, and not just because her teeth were chattering and she looked unsteady on her feet.

She blinked, and rain was on her eyelashes. "Come on, let's get inside." She turned and ran for the back door.

In the mudroom, he pried off his boots and she took off her shoes, her on the bench and him leaning against the opposite wall. He tried not to look at all the places her shirt was plastered to her skin, and didn't take off *his* shirt, though it was wet and sticky and cold.

"What are you going to do about your recipes getting stolen?" he asked, just trying to take his mind off of how good it had felt to have his hands on her waist. *Sorry, buddy,* he said to Rick, for maybe the hundredth time this week. He'd been doing his best to keep his distance from Morgan, but he'd found himself doing strange things he didn't recognize in himself, like, in the early mornings, pretending to be asleep when she walked past, just so he could see her shadow move across the room. He'd written lines in his songwriting notebook he hoped she'd never see.

She looked up from drying her feet with a towel. "Honestly, I don't know. Woods and Water basically stole months of work from me."

"Want me to run up there and pound some heads till we get some answers as to who's responsible?" He grinned.

She laughed. "Now, there's an elegant idea."

"We don't care about elegance, if something's effective. Seriously, I'll walk up there right now with you, if you want. Intimidate them some."

"Well, the chefs are coming to the tasting group in the morning. I think what I'll do is appeal to their sense of honor, you know? If I can get the mole to see the error of their ways, maybe they can help convince Woods and Water to stop serving those dishes. Not that I could use those recipes in the contest, because it's already stated online that they served them there. But, still, I've got to take a long view. Start creating new, secret recipes to use in the contest, and meanwhile get Woods and Water to use some common courtesy." She looked overwhelmed at the thought of it all.

Which really did make Jesse want to pound some heads. "Honor," he scoffed. "There's no honor among thieves, haven't you heard?" Then he saw something on the side of her neck. A dark, narrow thing, about two inches long. "Oh, Jesus!" he said, taking a step back. It looked like a leech, and he *hated* leeches. He wouldn't even go near water that had a threat of them. He didn't know how she'd gotten one on her up on the roof.

"What? What is it?"

"Hold real still." He steeled himself, reached for her. "Goddamn, I hope it hasn't attached itself real good."

"You hope *what* hasn't attached itself?" she said, frozen.

"Don't worry, I got it." He brushed her wet hair back and gently pulled her shirt collar away from her neck. He didn't want to alarm the thing and send it crawling into her hair.

"What are you *doing*, Jesse?" she said, still not moving.

He clenched his teeth, grabbed the thing and flung it to the floor, then snatched his boot and whammed it hard four times. When he stopped, an odd silence settled over the room, and he finally breathed, looking at the thing smashed on the floor. "That oughto do it," he said, shivering a little as he straightened up.

She burst out laughing. "What *was* that?" She crouched down to peer at the dead thing on the floor. "Aw." She picked it up and held it up toward him.

"Don't *touch* it. And don't put it up near me!"

"Poor little piece of bark. Guess you fixed it good." She was laughing again.

"Oh, my Lord." Weak with a strange mix of embarrassment and relief, he sank into a crouch next to her, shaking his head. He reached out and touched the piece of bark that she held between her fingers. "Here I thought I rescued you from a *leech*. My least favorite thing on earth, I will tell you."

She held his gaze for a moment, looking as if she had a thousand things on her mind and didn't know which one to say. Close to her – closer than he'd intended, and he wasn't sure how *that* had happened – he thought about how her wet hair and the warm skin of her neck had felt to his fingers, about how she'd looked smiling down at him from the roof and then coming down the ladder above him. He noticed how the open V of her white shirt stuck to her tan skin, forming a stark line that it was hard not to think about peeling back. He noticed that her mouth was wet with rain.

She suddenly stood up. "Well, thanks! I'm freezing! Going to go hop in the shower. Then I've got to get to work on those new recipes!"

Sorry, buddy, he told Rick again. "Good idea," he said, looking at his hands where he had them folded between his knees, and she was gone, with a soft sound of the door closing behind her.

He changed shirts and found his way to the attic to put down some tarps, then put his boots back on and grabbed the rain jacket he'd bought at Kayak Riot for a truly exorbitant price, though supposedly at an "end of season sale." He set out walking in the rain, and, for once, didn't mind the cold. He needed *something* to cool his blood.

What was the matter with him? Here he was, supposed to be helping Morgan, and instead he was having all these *thoughts* about her. And she wasn't wrong that he was bad news where women were concerned. Since Dawn, he'd never had a woman leave him. He'd left them all before they had a chance to.

And that was the last thing he'd ever want to see happen to Morgan. After the way she'd kept her heart in deep freeze since Rick, she deserved somebody who'd be there for her forever. Not to mention, he didn't even *like* her – a fact he was reminded of every night when he toted his guitar to this rock he'd found in the woods outside of town to play until it got dark and *he* got frozen through.

No, he was just plum straight up physically attracted to her, enough so that just about every other minute it slipped his mind that he didn't like her. And while that might not have stopped him from making a move on most women who he found as attractive as he did Morgan, and while some might say that his moral code with women had been on the loose side the past few years, one thing that was strictly off limits was "just for fun" sleeping with any woman who'd been the wife of his best friend.

He had to wonder, though – when she said there hadn't been anybody since Rick, did that mean she actually hadn't slept with anybody in six years? It hardly seemed possible.

Why, maybe if he did go to bed with her, he'd be performing a much-needed service, breaking her out of that shell she was clearly wearing over her heart and body. The way she'd looked at him, those thousand things on her mind, he was pretty sure at least one of them had to do with them taking off their clothes.

No, no loopholes, he cautioned himself, putting a stop to that line of thinking. *Sorry, buddy,* he told Rick. *Again.*

With that, Jesse decided: while he might not be the best guy on an everyday basis, he was going to be a good guy here and now. He was going to follow through on his promise to look after Morgan – in the way that a proper friend would.

Seemed like the least he could do was go find out about this Woods and Water deal. He didn't truck with waiting till tomorrow to find out who was stealing from Morgan.

Seconds after he let himself into Woods and Water's gleaming lobby, a New Jersey Housewife-type, all black hair and black eyeliner, emerged to greet him. "Look what the cat dragged in," she purred, leaning a curvaceous hip against the reception counter. Her black satin dress didn't leave much to the imagination, but Jesse doubted all of what he saw was God-given.

"Are you the owner of this place?"

"I sure am. Patty DuPage. What can I help you with, sugar?"

He didn't waste time. "You've been stealing Morgan's recipes. I'm here to tell you you'd better quit using them."

The woman pressed one long, painted talon to her lips. "Oh, dear. Are you threatening me? Accusing me with *no* evidence whatsoever, and then threatening me?"

Jesse was taken aback. "I'm just telling the truth."

"And you're here on behalf of Morgan Bailey, the owner of the Seacoast B&B?"

"That's right."

She grabbed a cell phone off the desk. To his shock, she held up the phone and it flashed; she'd taken his picture. She smiled coldly. "I'm texting my lawyer." She began tapping the screen with one long nail. "Telling him that Morgan Bailey sent hired muscle – in a cowboy hat – to intimidate me. To *scare* me, on a spooky, rainy evening, when *no one* else was around to witness it."

"Now, hold everything."

She looked up. "Or," she said, like she'd had a brainstorm. She set down the phone and took three slinky steps toward him, unbuttoning one top button of her dress. So few had been buttoned to begin with that the whole works threatened to give. Teal lace showed, and flesh. "Or you and I could be adults about this," she said, and she was near him, unzipping his rain jacket, laying a hand on his chest. "Imagine all that we could do…"

He pushed her hand away and stepped back. "Now, hold on."

She came after him. "Imagine all you could *tell* me."

He kept moving backward. "You've got the wrong idea."

"You know what's in *all* her secret sauces, I'll bet." Another button went.

"Lady, seriously."

"I've got some secrets of my own." She held open her dress so he had full view of that teal bra and everything in it.

He gave her a good, appreciative look. Why not? And then he couldn't help a sudden little laugh. "Not too well hidden, I reckon."

She scowled. Started buttoning up. "So, you don't want to handle this civilly. Then my lawyer it is. I hope *you* have a good one, because mine's a Rottweiler. You tell Morgan Bailey that hell's about to visit." She went for her phone again.

Jesse squared himself. "Morgan didn't send me, Mrs. DuPage. I came on my own. Now, you and I both know you're the one in the wrong, here. And I'm telling you to quit."

She scowled for a barely perceptible second, then batted her false eyelashes. "I have no idea what you're talking about."

"If you get your lawyer after me, I *will* get a good one – and I guarantee we *will* find evidence."

The woman rolled her eyes and sashayed off behind the desk. "I don't know what you're talking about. Anyway, even if we *were* serving dishes based loosely on Morgan's, there's nothing the least bit illegal about replicating a dish that someone else has cooked in the past. You can look it up."

He didn't like that one bit. "I'm talking about the principle of the thing. Of all the breakfasts in the world, why'd you have to serve her special ones?"

Patty stood on tiptoe, peering into the distance out the front windows. "I'm looking for that high horse you must've rode in on," she said. Then she lowered her feet and glared. "Why don't you get down off it?"

Jesse had to laugh – a little. But he'd been right about honor among thieves, and looking this woman in the face was giving him a stomachache. "Why don't *you* think about the consequences that your actions are having in other people's lives?"

She rolled her eyes. "Please. And, while you're at it, please leave. Before I decide you're trespassing and add that to your list of offenses."

There was no point in pushing his luck, since getting himself into trouble wouldn't help Morgan any. He moved for the door. "Think about what I said."

She smiled and pulled the front of her dress aside to show a small flash of teal. "Think about my offer."

"I think you are incorrigible," he told her, and went out into the night.

7

When he got back to Morgan's, she and Lainey were in the kitchen, Lainey sitting at the counter with a cup of tea, Morgan looking slightly crazed over a big mixing bowl full of just-cracked eggs. The counter was covered in fresh herbs, a pile of yams, and several kinds of cheese. "Breakfast for dinner, Jesse!" she said. "Bev said these were the last of her eggs, and, with the colder weather, her hens were laying slow. I don't know what I'll do if I can't get more eggs from her. I'll have to order from the mainland, and who knows how long that'll take."

"Calm down," Jesse said.

"Ha! I'd like to see *you* be calm under these circumstances. Where were you, anyway, in this rain?"

Jesse hated to, but he knew he had to tell her what he'd done. "Listen, about that," he said, and then he confessed, leaving out the part where Patty DuPage had threatened to call her lawyer.

Still, Morgan was not pleased. "You went up there and confronted her? Jesse!"

"I was trying to help."

"That's really sweet," Lainey said, her eyes sparkling as she sipped her tea.

"But, unfortunately, she's right," Morgan said. "There's nothing illegal about what she's done. And now, whoever her accomplice is, she'll warn them before they come tomorrow. So much for appealing to their sense of honor! She'll have already appealed to whatever she's been appealing to so far."

"Yeah, well, on that, I'd be looking at the *men* in that group. And that Mrs. DuPage, she's got no honor."

"Men. That's almost everybody, except Sam. Why? What happened?"

He just raised an eyebrow.

She frowned, understanding. "Oh. I've *heard* Mrs. DuPage likes to show off her assets. That's one consequence of her husband never paying attention, I guess."

"Seems that way."

Lainey set down her mug and stood up. "Listen, Morgan, I'd better be getting home. Brick got a Netflix in the mail today, and he made me promise we'd watch it. I think it's like six episodes of some series, so it'll take all night. And now that Jesse's here, he can be your taster." She grinned.

Morgan looked bewildered and a bit annoyed; Jesse couldn't guess why. "Well, okay. See you tomorrow morning?"

"Sounds good. Later, Jesse." With a cute little grin and wave, Lainey was gone.

A strange quiet descended. Morgan broke Jesse's gaze, picked up a whisk and began beating the eggs.

"Lainey," she said, "always drinks wine this time of night. Tonight she asked for tea. Very suspicious."

Jesse's eyebrows shot up. "What, you think she's pregnant?"

"Maybe. She won't say."

So Jesse's new buddy Brick might be about to become a dad. Jesse tamped down a quick flare of jealousy. "Listen, I'm going to go check out your attic and see if the tarps I put down are doing what they're meant to. It's still raining like a son of a gun out there."

"I checked a few minutes ago. Looks fine to me. Listen, are you hungry? I'm about to whip up three different breakfast ideas, and, well, like Lainey said, maybe you could be my taster."

He was surprised. "Me, with my 'refined palate'?"

She gave a little laugh. "At least I know you're not the mole." It was her turn to raise an eyebrow. "Unless Mrs. DuPage and her *assets* have lured you over to the dark side."

"No chance, I assure you."

"Then grab a beer out of the refrigerator, if you want," she said. So he did, and sat down on one of the stools at the island to watch her work.

Three hours later, the rain had slowed to a trickle, and he'd tried her savory herbed omelet, ham and zucchini quiche, and sweet potato hash with bacon brittle and poached eggs. He thought they were all great. "I guess I've been missing out!"

But Morgan wasn't satisfied. "Sweet breakfasts are really my forte, and sweet breakfasts always win these contests. I don't know why I even tried these. They are *unremarkable*." She sighed, scraping leftovers into Tupperware. "I can only hope that tomorrow we'll find out who's passed on the recipes. I might not win this contest, but I've at least got to save my business. God, what a mess. Do you think you can get the roof done in time, at least?"

"Well, with those stupid cedar shakes, there ain't no hurrying. Brick's been a help, but I need some more extra hands." He grinned, trying to take her mind off things. "Yours? You sure didn't seem to mind being up there today." He immediately regretted saying it – those damn flirting instincts of his had kicked in again.

She used the back of one wet hand to push a loose strand of hair out of her face. "Oh, hell, why not? I can probably spare about two hours tomorrow afternoon, if you can put up with showing me what to do. Then I have got to get the garden into shape. There are still some things left, since we haven't had a frost yet, but it would be good to pretty it up. It just occurred to me this judge might want to take pictures back there, too, since I get most of my ingredients from there."

"Does that mean the back of the roof needs to get done, too?"

Morgan's face fell. "Oh, God. I didn't even think of that."

"All right, let's just deal with one thing at a time. First off, I can help you with the garden during the hours when I can't be pounding on the roof. And, if you help with the roof, we'll get somewhere with both."

"You *garden*?"

"Morgan, I grew up on an organic farm before we knew to call it that."

"Oh! I guess I didn't know that. Well, that would be great. And maybe I should ask at the tasting group tomorrow if anyone else could help with the roof. The season's slowing down, so maybe people aren't working as much. Although, who knows, if we get the mole up there he might destroy my roof, too." She still looked overwhelmed. Exhausted.

Jesse felt pleased, though – more than he wanted to be – that they were finally getting along. He stood and brought his plate around to the sink. "Some more help'd be great, as long as they aren't idiots. I'm not sure any of that group qualifies."

She laughed.

"Listen," he said, "why don't you hit the hay? Let me clean up here. I know you'll be getting up at the crack of dawn, and I don't sleep that good, anyway, not playing my guitar."

Her face suddenly looked vulnerable, a little hurt. "Jesse, I'm sorry about that. You've been doing so much for me, and you came all this way... Listen, sometimes the Barnacle hires musicians. I'll ask Caroline Brooks, the owner, if she'd let you play there next week, all right?"

The news cheered him. "That'd be real nice. Thanks."

"Or, if you just want to sing, there's always karaoke night at the Cutthroat. Wednesdays and Saturdays, I think it is. I mean, you can't work *all* the time, right?"

"Well, you'd have to come *with* me for that," he blurted. "Show off that angel voice."

Her face clouded over. "That was a long time ago for me. And I *can* work all the time. I need to." Quick as that, she was back to the all-business, shelled-off Morgan he'd been seeing. "So, you really don't mind cleaning up? You worked hard today, too."

Damn those flirting instincts, sending her crawling back into her shell again. *Be her* friend, *remember?* "Got rained out, remember? And, by the way, you *can't* work all the time."

Her face softened a little. "Right. Well. Okay. Thanks." She seemed to have a thousand things on her mind again. "Good night, then." She turned to go.

"Good night," he said, watching her until she'd disappeared inside the French doors, and then he turned to the mountain of dishes. Without quite realizing it, he started to hum to himself, a fresh melody to go with words he hadn't written yet. He actually felt happy, to an extent that he couldn't remember feeling in years.

Holy hell, he thought, catching himself, realizing he hadn't thought about Rick in a couple of hours. He'd just been plain enjoying being in Morgan's company.

This had to stop.

He'd better try to talk to Tammy, remind himself of what he had waiting for him back in North Carolina. At least after he'd finished these dishes for Morgan.

By the time he got the kitchen clean, the clock showed past eleven, but he used Morgan's phone to dial Tammy's number. He got her voicemail. "Answer your damn phone," he said to it. "I'll call back in five minutes. I've got my cell phone off, so don't even try to text me."

As he was waiting, the books on Morgan's shelf near the phone caught his eye. One in particular, because it had her name on it. He pulled it off the shelf. She'd written a cookbook!

He paged through it, noticing it was from a few years back, and the recipes in it were far simpler than the ones she was experimenting with now. In fact, the first chapter was called "Back to Basics." He started reading and got caught up in her tale of how she'd moved to Seacoast for a simpler way of life, to be disconnected from the modern world, to appreciate the simple goodness of simple things. *I find that using ingredients that I've grown myself gives a sense of coming full circle, and in that way it brings me peace,* she'd written.

That sure didn't seem to be how she was approaching this contest, and, as he read, he wondered what had happened to change her.

When he read what she'd written about giving up her cell phone, that reminded him he was supposed to call Tammy. He put the book back on the shelf and dialed the number again.

She actually picked up. "It lives!" he said. Which might not have been the sweetest thing to say.

But never mind. She started in right away. "Jesse, you've been gone more than a week. When are you coming back?"

"Jesus, Tam. I'm in the middle of something, here. Helping out an old friend."

"Yeah, I heard that story when you left. But I'm bored. And I go out to the bars, and all these men are asking me to dance, and I say 'I have a boyfriend,' and they say, 'Dance with me, anyway,' and then they start telling me how they'd never leave me and how good they'd take care of me. And I can't help but wonder."

He didn't like the direction this was going. "And you're telling me this because?"

"Because I want to know what you're going to do about it."

He sighed. "Real question, I guess, is, what are *you* going to do?"

A thoughtful pause. "Depends how long you're going to be gone."

Jesse's stomach hurt. He wasn't sure, at a distance, how much he liked this girl, after all, and it was hard to think the roof would be done by Friday, like Morgan wanted, even if she did manage to find some more help for him.

"Listen, I'm tired," he told Tammy. "Let's talk about this another time."

"You're the one who called *me*."

"Good night, Tammy," he said, and hung up.

Man, this would all be so much easier if he actually wanted to go home.

8

"God, that's awful," said Uriah, his spiky red hair looking as affronted as the rest of him. The other chefs, gathered around Morgan's kitchen island, chimed in, agreeing. Lainey and Brick stood by Jesse, arms folded like enforcers. "Who would do such a thing?"

"I don't know," Morgan said. "Who would? It has to be one of you."

They all looked at each other. "Sure wasn't me," Paul said, stroking his graying-blond beard.

"Wasn't me," put in Ralph, his face flushing a shade darker than usual under his buzzed blond hair.

Morgan folded her arms, too. She'd already explained how much this meant to her; she'd promised that all would be forgiven if the mole just came clean and went with her to convince Woods and Water to stop using her ideas (though that wasn't totally true, because she would, of course, make sure the mole was fired from wherever he was working and made to leave the island).

Still, they all denied knowing, or having done, anything. "I know one of you must be cooking for them, too, because these dishes are complex," she added.

They looked at each other again, seeming mystified. "I'm sorry for you, Morgan," said Kevin, who with his gray hair and glasses looked more like a librarian than a chef, "but I don't know anybody who'd do anything like that."

She was about to tell them that she wasn't serving them anything this morning – she'd made a fresh batch of her old standby, blueberry pancakes, for her guests, and that was all, and her guests had already eaten and gone – when Jesse spoke up. "Listen, fellas, no hard feelings, all right? You can understand why Morgan would want to get to the bottom of this, but, if you say you're innocent, then you are." He glanced at Morgan, a glance that asked her to trust him. "Now, to make it up to you, why don't you all come to a campfire tonight? Say, eight o'clock. Free beer, and I'll be providing musical entertainment." He grinned like they were all his best friends. "Now, get on outa here for now."

They acted as if he'd just knighted them. Ha. If *she'd* been the one to tell them they weren't getting any breakfast this morning, they'd have gone away miffed.

Though she couldn't be too mad at Jesse. It had been so nice to wake up to a clean kitchen this morning, and he'd been so generous with his time last night. Not to mention, again, this morning, he looked good enough to cheer up any girl – though she was still doing her best not to notice that.

It took a while for the chefs all to say goodbye, to wish Morgan luck finding the culprit. "We'll get the bastard," said Uriah, in his seemingly permanent state of outrage. "I'll keep my ear to the ground," Brad promised, and both of them were so young – and Brad had such sincere, dewy brown eyes – that Morgan couldn't believe they could be the ones. Tom and Sam, who worked together at Brenneman's, the island's most upscale restaurant, wished her well and walked out holding hands. They'd been making eyes at each other all summer, and their romance had evidently blossomed. If Jesse's theory about Mrs. DuPage was true, that would seem to rule out Tom.

So if it wasn't Brad or Uriah, Tom or Sam, who was it? *None* of them seemed guilty to her – not big Ralph or librarian Kevin or kind, gray-bearded Paul.

When everybody except Brick and Lainey was gone, Morgan turned to Jesse. "And just how is entertaining everybody tonight going to help? Don't we have enough to think about?"

When he smiled, she felt it in her toes again, and wished she didn't. "The point is the free beer," he said. "Let 'em drink and their tongues get loose. You clearly weren't gonna get anywhere confronting them when they're stone-cold sober. I'll buy the beer and play music, so everybody'll stay longer, and you and Lainey and Brick can get to the bottom of things. The guilty guy's itching to confess, I guarantee it. Then you can get him off the island and get ole Woods and Water back to serving slop for breakfast."

"Good idea," Brick said. "I'm in." Lainey nodded.

Morgan sighed. "Fine. All right."

"Ready to get started, Brick?" Jesse said. Brick had said he'd help all morning on the roof, since today was Sunday, his day off, and Jesse had already checked the attic and found that last night's rain had done no damage to the inside of the house, so it wasn't like there was *no* good news.

"Let's get to it," Brick said, giving Lainey a quick, gentle kiss. Was he being extra sweet to her, or was that Morgan's imagination?

"Thanks, guys," Morgan said, watching the men walk out – and ignoring the squint-eyed smile that Lainey gave her. When the men were gone, she said to Lainey, "So, do *you* have any news?" She didn't want to feel jealous, but she did, a little.

"You'll be the first to know, if I do. Or, well, the second." Lainey grinned.

By afternoon, the only remnants of yesterday's storm were a few twigs and yellow leaves scattered across the sunny front lawn. Standing among them, Morgan held out her arms in a tent shape, holding her breath as Jesse, close in front of her, reached around her with a tool belt. When he'd walked past a moment before, he'd smelled so good she'd practically broken into a cold sweat, which was why she was holding her breath now, as his hands fumbled with the belt against her waist.

"Holy buckets," he said, "you're too skinny. There's no hole where you need one." He took the belt off her and laid it out on the grass, getting his hammer and a nail from his own belt. "All that food you make. Don't you ever eat any of it? You oughto be two hundred pounds."

Morgan took in oxygen while she had the chance and tried to keep her mind on what was important. This morning, she'd rifled through her cookbooks trying to come up with new twists on sweet breakfasts, but she was still feeling at a loss, which wasn't like her at all. "So you didn't see *anything* this morning to lead you to suspect anyone in particular?" she asked Jesse.

He positioned the nail over the belt and whacked it with the hammer. "Like I told you, to me, they're *all* squirrely. Here we go." He stood up.

"Probably because you blew our cover last night," she said, then held her breath again as he came near – "Whatever," he muttered – and wrapped the belt around. By the time he fastened it, she *had* to take a breath, which meant she got another whiff of him, this one even more affecting than before. He'd been working outside all morning and part of the afternoon, and the air was just cool enough so he wasn't exactly sweaty, but he smelled of exertion and cedar, autumn and earth and soap.

Just her luck that she'd be attracted not only to how he looked but also to how he smelled. Damn pheromones. She tried to think about crepes and waffles, anything that would actually seem novel to a *Simple Food* judge who'd probably seen everything. She tried to decide which of the chefs had acted guilty this morning, but still came up with nothing.

Jesse gave the belt a tug. "She's secure, I'd say."

Morgan huffed in pretend exasperation. "Why do men always use 'she' to refer to a thing?"

He grinned. "Only to things that confound us, or that we'd like to fix."

She shook her head. "It's a good thing you're such a Neanderthal."

"Yeah, or what?"

Her face heated up. She hadn't meant to let on to being so attracted to him.

Time for a change of subject. She looked up. The main part of the roof was shingled all the way to the top. "It looks like you got a lot done this morning."

He looked up, too, assessing. "Yeah, well, I've still got some corners, and those'll be a small nightmare, but Brick helped this morning, and Paul signed on for tomorrow. Said he had a little experience." He looked at her, his blue eyes intense, his mouth thin. "Maybe you could ask some more people. Brick was telling me that people are always willing to help each other out here. Anybody with a little knowledge would be great. You, I'm letting help just so you'll have some idea why these cedar shakes take so dang long. Speaking of. Want to go ahead up?"

Relieved to get some distance from the way her knees wobbled when he turned those eyes on her, she went over, and he came to hold the scaffolding for her again. His hand brushed hers as he moved in behind her, and her body reacted again.

She reined the feelings in. This was not the time to get weak-kneed. This was the time to be thinking about pancakes and soufflés. Anyway, this was *Jesse*. It was like she kept forgetting who he was. And who *she* was, for that matter.

Which brought her back to the problem at hand. "I just can't believe you invited the chefs to a *campfire*," she called down. "I don't know *what* I'm going to serve."

"Just put out some marshmallows and relax. Point is to get people a little drunk so they start telling the truth about things, remember?"

Morgan clambered up onto the platform, thinking she'd have to remember not to drink very much herself, or this issue of her weak knees might come out. Which could *only* be a product of her not having been alone with an attractive man in all these years.

From the platform, the view of the blue harbor surrounded by the changing leaves of autumn was so gorgeous it was stunning. Not too often did she take the time truly to register her surroundings – especially not when she had pressing problems with the B&B. And, come to think of it, something about the B&B was *always* preoccupying her. Whether it was a *Simple Food* contest, or being convinced she wouldn't survive without adding two new bathrooms, or deciding this room or that just *had* to be redecorated (something she'd done more times than she could count). Was any of it *that* important, in the great scheme of life? Maybe not.

She hated to think it was Jesse who was making her appreciate the world's beauty a little more, but she knew it was. Strange, really, when he came across as such an insensitive smartass.

"I'm coming up!" he yelled, and she was glad, and soon he was on the platform beside her, smelling just as good as he did on the ground and showing her how to tell the froe-end of a shake, how to position the felt interlay, and exactly where to pound the two nails each shake required. Soon, they were both at work, pounding in synchronous strokes that vibrated pleasantly through

Morgan, as she relished the feeling of being, for the moment, high above the world and her worries – and of sharing that carefree space with Jesse.

"But, I mean, how do you *feel* about him?" Lainey said in low voice, leaning close to Morgan in the light of the campfire. Having decided to wait till people had had more to drink before they started asking questions, they were sitting on rocks in Morgan's backyard, roasting marshmallows.

"Shh!" Morgan said.

Quite a crowd had assembled, not just the chefs, as word had spread that Morgan was hosting a party. On Lainey's other side sat her assistant, Hannah Champlain, who was twenty-five and so pretty in her designer outfits – tonight she was decked out in an expensive-looking down vest, high-end jeans, and extravagant leather riding boots – instinct was to hate her.

But the Champlains had helped save Lainey's business (that was just after Hannah's younger brother, Hunter, had hit on Lainey last summer when she was bereft thinking things weren't going to work out with Brick, but that was a whole other story). And Hannah was hilarious, spunky, and as dark as she was sweet.

Just then, Jesse walked past, carrying his guitar. He gave Morgan a small smile that nevertheless showcased his dimple, and went to sit on the other side of the fire.

Hannah let out a low whistle. "If I were into cowboys, and if I weren't practically engaged, I'd be all into him. Yippee ki yay."

"I think *Morgan* might be into cowboys," Lainey whispered. "There are serious sparks between these two."

"You're practically engaged, Hannah?" Morgan said. "Tell me about that." Anything to deflect attention. Besides, she hadn't spent too much time with the girl till now; summer had been so busy.

Hannah seemed happy for the attention. "Oh, well, my boyfriend, Matt, he's a trader on Wall Street, and we've been apart since I moved out here, and he says he just can't stand it anymore. I'm going down to New York in two weeks, and he says he has a big surprise. We've been together two years, so, you know. Sorry, Lainey, but I probably won't be back next summer."

"You've said. I don't know what I'll do without you."

Morgan pulled her marshmallow out of the fire, and, after a moment, popped it into her mouth. Swallowing the gooey goodness and licking her fingers, she glanced at Jesse across the campfire. His eyes met hers. She looked away, her face getting hot.

Like she was in high school, for God's sake! Not that she'd been this bad even in high school. At least then she'd had the brains not to be attracted to an unapologetic ladies' man like Jesse. She sent Rick another small apology, though it suddenly occurred to her to wonder if he really would mind, after all this time.

"Yippee ki yay," Hannah said again with a grin.

Lainey polished off her marshmallow. "Listen, I know he was Rick's best friend," she whispered, wiping her fingers on the grass. "But he's really hot, he clearly likes you – and Rick's been gone a long time."

That brought reality crashing back to Morgan. No way was she in high school. She was a 33-year-old widow who'd lost the love of her life. Of *course* Jesse was off limits. "I know how long Rick's been gone. Besides, I don't even *like* Jesse. And he doesn't like me. Except as friends, I mean. Anyway, he's got a girlfriend back home. Yes, he's being really sweet and helping me out, but that's all."

Lainey reached for her cup of tea. "Right."

"I know!" Hannah said. "We send the girlfriend a gift basket of cake pops. Unsigned. She thinks it's from him. It isn't. She's all like, 'Why don't you ever send me anything?' And things just start to freaking unravel."

Lainey laughed. "Cake pops?"

"Either that or one of those edible arrangements. Something slightly phallic, anyway."

Morgan couldn't help laughing, too. "We are not sending any gift baskets. Anyway, there's nothing between me and Jesse. Nothing."

On the other side of the fire, Jesse cleared his throat and started strumming his guitar. The crowd quieted. "Well, thanks, y'all, for coming. Help yourself to the marshmallows and beer. I'm just gonna play you a couple little songs of mine."

The song's opening chords were haunting, and, when his clear voice rang out, Morgan shivered like she'd been visited by a ghost. But it wasn't the past affecting her. It was Jesse's voice, snaking under her skin in a way that nothing had in years.

The feeling was terrifying – and irresistible. So she just listened, letting his voice transport her.

The song was about a lonely man coming to understand that his love affair was over because he couldn't be the kind of man his girl needed him to be. A perfect song for Jesse, in other words. Morgan held her breath when he sang the high notes and swallowed a lump in her throat when he sang about his broken heart. By the last notes, she'd shed some tears, and, when the crowd burst into applause and cheers, she took a second to join in.

Lainey, applauding, leaned into her shoulder. "Nope, nothing there at all."

Morgan wiped her face. "Shut up." Had anyone else noticed? It didn't look like it, thank goodness. She put on a smile and kept clapping.

"Thank you so much," Jesse said modestly, waiting for the cheers to die down. "Why don't y'all have another beer?" And then he launched into another song, George Strait's "Amarillo by Morning." One of Morgan's favorite country songs, about travelling alone with everything you owned. Another lonesome cowboy song.

Bev Hargrove came and sat down on Morgan's other side. "He's *good*," she said, which was a high compliment coming from the woman who was the island's resident ex-hippie folk singer.

"Yes," Morgan said. That word hardly conveyed all the things his voice was making her feel.

"Though no Dylan, of course." Bev was a dyed-in-the-wool Bob Dylan fan, and no one would ever measure up in her eyes.

Morgan laughed. "Of course."

"Now, I can get you a dozen more eggs by tomorrow, but, if you're gonna need more than that, I'm afraid you're gonna have to find another source."

"Okay, Bev, thanks. I'll figure something out." Morgan saw Brick talking to dewy-eyed Brad and big Ralph, and hoped he was getting somewhere. Then she saw Caroline Brooks and remembered her promise to ask her about hiring Jesse for a gig at the Barnacle. She explained to Lainey and Hannah, who both grinned. She rolled her eyes, then got up and went over. When she made the request, Caroline grinned, too. "This guy? We'd be honored. But not until Friday night, okay? We won't be busy enough this week. I pay a hundred dollars."

One night didn't seem like enough. Besides, Jesse was planning to leave on Friday. "What if he wanted to come in and play for free every night? He's been just dying to play, and I haven't wanted him to disturb my guests."

"I'd rather keep it a special thing for Friday," Caroline said. "Columbus Day weekend and all. We'll have him play at nine, so people who finish eating will stay for drinks."

Despite Morgan's best efforts, Caroline wouldn't change her mind. "All right," Morgan finally said, and squeezed Caroline's elbow to thank her. One night was better than nothing. And if Jesse didn't want to stay the extra day, he could always decline.

Though, at the rate it was going, the roof would probably still need work.

With the thought of him staying longer, Morgan found herself enthusiastic. She didn't want to think what that might mean.

She turned back to watch him play. He was in the middle of another George Strait song, "Troubadour," and made a gorgeous picture in the firelight, his face shadowed by his hat. She started to hum along, then caught herself. No way was she going to let herself start singing.

In fact, she really should be in the kitchen right now, coming up with new recipes – ones that didn't require too many eggs, apparently.

But she supposed she could at least tell Jesse about the gig at the Barnacle. Tell him maybe he should stay a little longer, and see what he'd say about that.

9

Jesse always felt at home when he had his guitar. Even when he'd been in the desert. It was what had saved him over there, he truly believed. The sound of his own music.

But when he was nearing the end of "Troubadour" and looked up and saw Morgan gazing at him across the flickering campfire, he just about choked on his own breath, and he had all he could do to finish the song. Fortunately, people started applauding before he lost the last note to a crack in his voice.

With effort, he broke her gaze and smiled at the crowd. "Time for a little break, folks." He set down his guitar to good-natured boos and a little laughter.

As he was standing up, he heard her voice. "Jesse, I've got good news!"

He got her in his sights. She was smiling – and looking even more stunning up close than she had across the fire.

"Caroline Brooks wants you to play on Friday at the Barnacle," she said.

"Friday night?" This was undeniably good news, but… "I told you I'd be outa your hair on Friday."

"Don't worry. Stay an extra day. Anyway, she said she'll pay a hundred dollars. I know it isn't much, but…"

"You're sure you don't mind?"

"Of course not."

He took off his hat, put it back on and straightened it, processing the whole deal. "Well, that's cool," he said, in a gigantic understatement. He'd always wanted to think he was good enough to earn *money* playing music. "That'll be my first paid gig."

Her mouth fell open a little. "You're kidding. You're so *good*."

He grinned at that. "Been a little busy fighting terrorists. But thanks. That's sweet." Her eyes were bright and mesmerizing in the firelight. He didn't want to look away.

"Hey, Jesse!" This was Uriah, breaking in. "Do you take requests?"

Morgan gave Jesse a little smile and turned away, leaving him only half listening to Uriah's request. His gaze followed Morgan back to the other side of the fire and through the crowd, and he watched as she disappeared inside the house.

Wishing she'd stayed, and not certain why she wouldn't – she was the reason for the party, after all – he played another set before people started to drift away. Then there were long good nights and "hope to hear you again"s and thank yous and "next time at my place"s. There were empty bottles to gather and a fire to put out, and he kept wondering where she was.

Lainey and Brick helped clean up, and Lainey introduced him to her assistant, Hannah, who told him within about thirty seconds that in two weeks she was heading back to New York City to be with her boyfriend and work on placing her jewelry designs, which had been selling well all summer at the bookstore, in boutiques there. She showed him a ring she was wearing that she'd made of sterling silver and a single green topaz. "That's awesome," he said, and meant it. It was beautiful and unique, rugged and delicate at once.

Hannah smiled. "Thanks! Stop by if you want to see what I've got for sale."

Lainey and Brick were the last to leave. "Tell her we tried our damndest," Brick said. "They're a pretty discreet bunch. Or, at least, whoever it is doesn't have a crack in his façade."

"Hey, guys," Jesse said. "I was just wondering. Is it true Morgan really hasn't dated anybody since she's been out here on the island? Six years or so?"

"As far as we know," Brick said.

Lainey smiled and touched Jesse's elbow. "Talk to her," she said, with a certain urgency, but, as the pair turned to go, Jesse wasn't sure what she'd meant by that; what, exactly, he was supposed to talk to Morgan *about*.

When he went inside, she was sitting at the computer in the kitchen, making notes on a scratch pad. She looked up when she heard him and smiled. "Trying to get inspired," she said, and it was a kind of apology.

Still, he didn't like that she hadn't stayed at the fire. It could only mean she hadn't liked his singing. "Brick and Lainey didn't find out squat," he said. "Sorry."

Her smile faded. "Oh." Then she brightened again. "Hey, Jesse, what would you think of cinnamon custard baked French toast with poached pears and fig sauce?"

Clearly, thinking about these recipes made her far happier than anything else did, and that seemed so lonely it made him sad. Not wanting to let on, he gave a long, low whistle. "Holy buckets, is what I'd think. You ever think you're trying too hard?"

She cocked her head. "No."

"I *would* point out that this judge is from a magazine called *Simple Food*. Of course, I'm a simple man, so I could be wrong, but I would think they're looking for 'simple food.'"

"Oh." She looked confused, seemed at a loss for words.

He thought of Lainey's telling him that he needed to talk to her. But what could he say? "Well, I'm about to hit the hay. You need to get some sleep, too."

"But I was thinking of trying this for breakfast tomorrow, so I have to make sure I've got what I need."

"It's after midnight."

She rolled her eyes and blew out air. "Fine. In a few minutes. I think you're right and I should look at the *Simple Food* website, see what kinds of things they think are good."

"Now, Morgan. Or you'll get swallowed up by the Google monster, I'm afraid, and end up sitting here till three a.m."

She raised an eyebrow. "All right. I suppose you're right. Morning's going to come early, and I still have to wash the smoke out of my hair." She shut the lid of her computer, got up and came over by him. "I liked your playing tonight."

"Yeah, so much you didn't even stick around. Though I do appreciate you getting me that gig at your friend's place."

"That was my pleasure. And I did enjoy your music. I just realized I needed to stop feeling sorry for myself and get to work."

"I haven't seen you feeling sorry for yourself yet." He held open the French door, and she smiled and went ahead of him.

"Good night," she said in the darkness, and he wished he had more he could say in return, and then she was gone, her door shutting behind her.

Upstairs brushing his teeth, Jesse remembered something. Uriah, talking to him. Jesse had asked where all the chefs worked and Uriah had listed them off – Tom and Sam and Kevin at Brenneman's; Brad at the Barnacle; Ralph and Paul at the Island Inn; Uriah himself at the Cutthroat Tavern ("Burgers and grilled fish sandwiches, all summer long, man"). Then Uriah had mentioned that Ralph's hours at the Island Inn had been cut back since Labor Day and nobody knew quite what he was doing with his time or how he was making money. He claimed to be taking photographs to build his following on Instagram, which he thought could lead to a job in Boston or New York.

Without cell signal? Jesse thought now. *Where's he getting his internet?*

He thought he should tell Morgan, so, when he went downstairs, he tapped on her bedroom door.

No answer. But he didn't think she could possibly be asleep yet, and he knew she'd want to hear this. He tapped again and opened the door a crack. "Morgan?"

He heard the shower running – and heard her singing. An Alison Krauss song he knew, "Whenever You Come Around."

Her voice was so beautiful that it gave him chills and about broke his heart at once.

Yet there was something unconscious about her singing, too, as if she wasn't even *aware* she was singing. Was her voice just needing to be heard that much, that it would come out on its own, when she wasn't paying attention?

He listened for a moment, the notes seeping through him like good wine, giving him a pleasant sense of floating, almost dizziness, and a little chill under his skin. Then he caught himself. He couldn't let himself get affected like this.

He stepped back and shut the door, feeling like he'd seriously breached her privacy, without meaning to. His news could wait till tomorrow.

Guilty as he felt for hearing her when she probably hadn't meant to be heard, he was already plotting ways he could get her to sing in public again. And get her to sing with *him.* He wanted to know what it would be like to have that angel voice – that voice that so clearly needed to be heard – blending with his.

To be right next to her, so that he could not just hear but *feel* it.

10

In the middle of the dark night, Morgan woke up to an odd, strangled cry. She was immediately wide awake, frightened.

What *was* that? Some cat or something, outside?

The noise came again.

From inside the house.

From the next room.

Jesse's voice, making sounds without words.

A nightmare? Or something worse?

She threw back the covers, jumped up and ran for him.

He was sprawled on the couch on his back, his arms over his face as if to protect it. Again, the blanket covered only his midsection, and the large, smooth contours of his bare chest and legs and arms showed in the moonlight.

"Jesse? Are you all right?"

He made another strange noise. Was he choking? Having a seizure? Should she try to turn his head?

How? With those heavy arms on top of it? And, if he *was* having a nightmare, he might perceive anything she did as a threat and attack. She'd had *that* training before

Rick had come home from deployment. The time he had come home.

Praying Jesse *was* just sleeping, she grabbed a pillow and threw it at his arms. "Jesse, wake up!"

His arms flailed. "What?" He snorted, then sat up, his eyes wide open, looking frightened and ready for action.

"Jesse, it's all right," Morgan said, backing away slowly. "You were having a dream. You're here in Maine with me. Morgan."

He blinked a few times, coming back to reality. His face softened. He rubbed his forehead with both hands. "Goddamn."

"Are you all right?"

"I didn't mean to scare you. Wake you up."

The vulnerability on his face unsettled her, but she didn't want to let on. And the memory of last night was returning. Jesse, after the campfire, insisting she get some sleep. She couldn't remember the last time anyone under her roof had been concerned about her welfare; usually *she* was the one taking care of everybody else. And then the way he'd thanked her again for lining up the gig for him, and said good night with that look she couldn't quite identify – somewhere between mystification and ruefulness, sorrow and joy.

And God only knew how *she'd* been looking at *him*.

Or how she was looking at him now. She caught herself. "I'm just sorry you had a bad dream. Can I get you anything?"

"No. Thanks."

"A cup of tea might help relax you. Help you get back to sleep. I might need some myself!" She laughed a little, trying to lighten the mood.

He rubbed his face again. "Okay. Thanks."

She went to the kitchen and put the kettle on. By the time she went back into the living room with two steaming cups, he'd covered his whole lower half with the blanket – a small disappointment – and was sitting on one end of the couch. "Sit here with me," he said, taking a cup from her. He seemed peaceful now, but sad, so she sat down cross-legged at the other end, understanding what it was like not to want to be alone. She held her tea in both hands, blowing across the top to cool it.

"Do you ever dream about him?" Jesse said, surprising her.

She spoke carefully. "Sometimes. Not as often as I used to." She never talked to anyone about this. "Either way – if I dream about him or I don't – it's a little heartbreak."

Jesse nodded slowly. "I understand."

"Were you dreaming about him?"

"I don't want to talk about it."

"Okay." She sipped her tea. He rubbed his forehead again.

She said, "I thought when you played music it helped you sleep better."

That got a rueful smile. "That ain't foolproof." A pause, and then a look came over his face like he'd had an idea. "Hey, can I ask you something?"

She nodded.

"What do you think your life would be like now, if he was still here?"

"Oh!" Something she didn't let herself think about, normally. But Jesse was looking at her with the hopefulness of a child. "Well, we probably wouldn't live on Seacoast. Maybe we'd have stayed in Wilmington. We liked it there. He wanted to go into management, and I'd've probably stayed on with my band, or maybe opened my own bakery." She got wistful. "We'd've had kids by now."

Jesse face showed his surprise. "Kids? Really? You don't seem the type. Rick never mentioned it."

She tried not to be offended. "What makes you say that? We wanted three. Rick wanted to start right away, but I said we should wait till he was done with the Marines. I thought our life could really start, then." It was one of her biggest regrets – not having a child to carry on a part of him. "Oh, Jesse, why did you have to talk him into re-enlisting that last time?"

Jesse's eyebrows shot up. "Me? Boy, you got that story wrong. It was the other way around. He convinced *me*. Said we couldn't leave our men to go it alone when the war was nowhere close to over."

She didn't want to believe that. Couldn't. Her wedding ring felt heavy on her hand. "But he told me..."

Jesse shook his head. "He didn't want you to think he didn't want to be with you. He did. You were all he talked about. But, you know, the Marines were important, too. He believed in doing his duty."

"So he wasn't going to quit, even after that tour."

"Not likely. I'm sorry."

Morgan felt the shock of a long-held and precious belief deflating. "Oh. Wow. I wish he'd told me." She sipped her tea, trying to stay calm, then blurted, "I would've gone ahead and had his baby! If he was just going to keep on being a Marine, anyway. God, I feel like an idiot now. I was so mad at you."

Jesse smiled. "Well, you can quit that."

She laughed a little, though she was hurt. Rick hadn't exactly *lied* to her, but when she'd jumped to her own conclusions about why he'd re-enlisted – she remembered their huge fight the day he'd told her – he'd let her believe that it had been Jesse's idea.

She forgave Rick now, instantly, of course – he'd been just a human being, bound to have faults like anyone else.

Just like Jesse had said, that first fight they'd had, when he'd made her so mad saying that Rick would've disappointed her eventually.

Now Jesse looked sideways at her. "But you're not... you know, into *family* things. Was having a family all Rick's idea?"

"No! No, I always wanted kids. I only have one sister, ten years older, so growing up was lonely. So I wanted several, all close in age. And he did, too, because he liked growing up with his brother and sister."

"But, I mean, Rick's folks told me they invited you to Thanksgivings and Christmases and such, and you never went."

"Oh, my God. Seriously? *This* is where you're getting this from?"

"Their feelings were really hurt. We all thought you were just plum over the whole deal."

"Are you kidding me?" She wiped away sudden tears at the insinuation – and at the memory of getting those invitations; how cold she must have sounded on the phone, turning them away. "How was I supposed to stand it? Going to his *parents'* house for *Christmas*? Without him?"

"Oh." Jesse seemed stunned.

"Knowing that the whole dream of life that I'd had was gone with him? We used to talk about having Christmas with his parents and our *children*, for God's sake!"

Silence fell; Jesse wouldn't meet her eyes. He took a drink of his tea, then winced like it was too hot. He set it on the coffee table in front of him. "I've always wanted kids, too. Two or three, I guess. Me and Dawn used to talk about it. I haven't wanted to talk to anybody about it since."

She was relieved he'd changed the subject – and surprised. "You? Mr. Ladies' Man?"

He winced again. "You know, Morgan, sometimes things happen in life that make a person seem a way they're really not."

She gave a short, surprised laugh. "Tell me about it. Well, I don't think Dawn would've been the best choice as a mother to your children. But you have plenty of time to find someone. Not me. That ship's sailed for me."

He sat up straight and turned his gaze on her full-blast. "What do you mean? You're only, what, thirty-three years old?"

She shrugged. "My life is set here. Besides, when there's only one person in the world who makes the world be what it is, and then suddenly that person's gone..."

Jesse interrupted. "I'm sorry, but that's a load of crap. You're going to consider your life over?"

"Don't tell me what it's like to go through what I've been through."

"Everybody goes through stuff in life. They don't let it stop them from living."

"I *am* living. Just a different life than the one I would've had with Rick."

"He wouldn't want you to give up on your dreams, I'm fairly sure."

"How do *you* know what he'd want for me? For that matter, how do you know that my dreams haven't changed? They *do* that, you know."

He held up his hands, conceding slightly. "I'm just saying, if you think you want kids, you shouldn't let life pass you by."

"Your objection is noted," she said coldly, because she didn't like the way she must seem to him now. She'd have thought he'd be happy that she was being faithful to the memory of his friend. Instead, he seemed to think she was pathetic.

To her surprise, though, he grinned. "You've got to admit, Morgan, maybe it's a good thing I showed up."

She set her tea down and gathered her hair, twisting it into a bun, just for something to do with her hands. "Why?"

"Break you out of your rut."

She let her hair fall. "I'm not in a rut," she said, though of course she was.

Had been, anyway.

He reached over to lay one big, warm hand on her knee. "Morgan, it's all right," he said, with a sudden gentleness that all but broke her in two.

Forget about being concerned for her welfare – how long had it been since any man had offered her comfort? Or touched her, other than a handshake?

Her alarm and vulnerability must have shown on her face. "I know," Jesse said, smiling at her the way you'd smile at a child who'd scraped her knee.

Tears filled her eyes. She wiped them away. "You're a good friend, Jesse," she said, reminding herself again. He was her husband's best friend. (Even if she couldn't still be mad at him for making Rick re-enlist, since he hadn't.) "I can see that now."

Regret flashed across his face, and he pulled his hand back. She missed its heat immediately. He grinned again. "Never understood what he saw in me, did you?"

She laughed. "No, I didn't." *Friends, friends, friends,* she said to herself, a refrain to keep her sane. Still, when she looked at him, at the way his skin stretched over his muscles and his hair curled over his ears, she saw how truly beautiful he was. And, she was realizing, not just on the outside.

Her eyes slid over him until they found his.

"I don't know why, either," he said.

The non-sequitur confused her. "What?"

"Why it was him and not me. Why he couldn't have come home to you. I didn't have anything to come home to. It should've been me."

Her heart broke that he would feel this way – and that he'd assume it was what she was thinking, too. She didn't know what to say. "Oh, Jesse." She gave in to the desire to reach out and press her hand to his chest, as if to comfort him. Though maybe she was the one who needed comforting.

She could feel his heart beating, strong in his solid chest. "You have such a good heart." She could feel that, too, suddenly. "Thank you for being here."

He pressed his hand over hers, and his eyes were the softest she'd seen them. "I'm getting the notion that you have a good heart, too, Morgan."

She was conscious of him looking at her mouth. And that she was looking at his.

Was he right that she needed to move on from her grief?

Surely he hadn't meant with him. Surely *he* knew how wrong that would be – even if she might be on the road to forgetting it in this particular moment.

What should I do, sweetheart? she asked, but this time she got no answer from Rick.

And they'd never talked about it – the question of what she'd do if he didn't make it home. She'd never wanted to speak the possibility out loud. Was Jesse right that Rick wouldn't want her to be living with her heart closed off?

She remembered Rick's cute little sheepish smile, the one he'd given her when he thought she might be mad. The way his ears stuck out a little too much under the shaved sides of his military haircut. The deep, sweet brown of his eyes. He'd loved to play Frisbee in the park. Wanted her to grow her hair longer. Wanted her to sing. Wanted to get a puppy, timed so their first child would grow up with it. (Had he thought he'd be able to convince her to have a baby even if he stayed in the Marines? Maybe he had. Maybe he'd had dreams completely different from hers, and would have revealed them in time.) Above all, she thought, he'd wanted her to be happy....

And he'd loved Jesse like a brother.

That part was all just too strange. Especially since Jesse wasn't someone she could ever have a *relationship* with. They were too different; their lives were too different. He was set on taking over his father's business in North Carolina, and she was firmly rooted here.

So what she was considering here, tonight, apparently was just getting physical with him.

Really, really physical.

She pulled her hand from under his.

It couldn't happen.

But she missed his heat on her palm. Energy hummed between them, and felt like possibility.

No: she wouldn't yield to a misguided middle-of-the-night temptation that she would only deeply, deeply regret tomorrow.

"I think I'd better go back to bed," she said.

His mouth tightened for an instant. "Good idea."

That settled it, and seemed good, because she didn't know what she'd have done if he'd protested.

As she got up, he stretched out on the couch, getting himself settled in – which hardly made him less alluring. She felt heat in parts of her that she'd nearly forgotten existed, and tried to shut them down.

"Hey, thanks," he said. "For… you know, being cool about the nightmare and all. And for the tea! Oh, and remind me in the morning, Uriah said something interesting about Ralph."

"Okay, great," she said, not wanting to think about all that now, or it might keep her awake.

Goodness, he was beautiful, the shape of his mouth, the slope of his nose.

Good thing he was leaving in a week, or who knew how long her restraint would last?

And giving in to her desire would only hurt them both in the long run. He'd leave, of course, and they'd probably both be so embarrassed that they'd never speak again.

She didn't want that. Because losing Jesse's friendship would mean losing a line that tethered her to Rick, to the past.

In fact, she'd been so careful to sever most of them that Jesse might be the only one she had left.

That *really* settled it. "And, you know, what are friends for?" she said, and she left him.

11

"Seriously, Morgan, we got the garden in good shape the last couple days, and the roof's getting close, too, with all the help I've been getting," Jesse said, taking another big bite of his BLT. He'd come to count on having two every day for lunch. He didn't know what special touch Morgan added to them, but they were the best BLTs he'd had in his life, and he didn't think he'd ever get tired of them.

He also didn't think that, even with help, he'd finish the roof by Friday, only two days away, but he wasn't going to bring that up now. "I think you can take one night off."

Morgan grabbed a carton of eggs from the refrigerator. "I don't think so. I've got less than a week till Ally comes, and three recipes to come up with and perfect. Being 'simple' and still being outstanding is a challenge, for sure. I've been looking at the *Simple Food* website, and I got three dozen eggs from the mainland this morning, so I can actually practice some ideas. I cleaned the rooms the quickest I ever have, this morning." She brushed her hair off her face and sighed. "But I'm still not feeling that inspired."

As always, looking at her, how gorgeous she was, Jesse had to work not to basically pass out. And, as always, he pretended not to be affected. "Ally, that's the judge?"

"Yes, and she's been emailing me saying she's got high expectations."

"You wouldn't be a finalist if she didn't." Jesse grinned, and Morgan rolled her eyes, then pulled out a stick of butter and a carton of milk.

After Jesse's nightmare the other night of Rick and him and a bunch of guys in the desert, just walking along, and then a sudden explosion, and everyone turning to blood and bone; after Morgan had put her hand over his heart and he'd somehow, somehow, by the skin of his teeth, kept himself from pulling her to him, he'd been reminding himself non-stop who she was, who he was. He'd been working as hard as he could on the roof and the garden, not wanting to leave her in the lurch with half the roof still to do before winter, but figuring the sooner he got out of here and away from her and all the feelings she was stirring up in him, the better.

But that didn't mean he wasn't still going to try to get her to sing with him. "Come on. Karaoke tonight would be fun. You could use a little fun. Let your subconscious mind work on the problem."

She sat down at the computer, opened the internet, typed something in. "I bet Lainey and Brick would go with you."

"I want *you* to go with me."

She was glaring at the screen. "Shit."

"What's wrong?"

"Woods and Water's serving another new breakfast. Cinnamon roll-pecan waffles with cranberry-peach sauce! I made that for the tasting group last month, and I was thinking of resurrecting it, seeing if it was simple enough. I'd thought it was *too* simple. But they even figured out my secret ingredient. They have a whole little article about it: 'The Secret is in the Sauce!' With an exclamation point."

She looked so upset that he wanted to go over and give her a hug. He stayed on his stool. "What's the secret?"

"Key lime. Just a little. They even got the amount almost right." She slumped in her chair. "I don't understand how this is happening."

Jesse put down his sandwich. "All right, listen. Just because the first lead we got the other night didn't amount to beans doesn't mean we can't still find out who's doing this." Some minor investigation had turned up that Ralph really *was* spending his days taking photographs – Bev Hargrove had said that her hens and their many-colored eggs were one of his favorite subjects, and he spent a couple hours in the coop every day. His Instagram page showed he was posting several times a day and had amassed thousands of followers. He was evidently using the dial-up internet at the Island Inn, which was so slow that uploading photos accounted for the rest of his time. "Forget karaoke tonight," Jesse said. "We've got to host another bonfire."

Briefly, Morgan leaned her head in her hands. When she looked up, her jaw was set and her eyes were hard. "All right." She stood, twisting up her hair and going for the phone. "But this time we're not going to take a subtle approach. This time we're going to come right out and ask the whole island to help us find this rat."

Most people arrived around eight, yawning and saying they weren't used to being out this late on a weeknight. "Only when somebody needs help do we go out at night," Bev told Jesse, "and Morgan said this was serious." Jesse was getting to know them all: Lainey and Brick, Bev, Jack and Deborah Harrison (they owned the Island Inn), Caroline Brooks of the Barnacle, and Hannah Champlain. Then there was an old, white-bearded lobsterman named Caleb Brown, who claimed to creak when he moved, and Tim Sawyer, a grungy lobsterman in his late thirties, who joked he'd soon be doing the same.

The chefs wouldn't arrive till after they were done with work, around nine, so when everyone else was settled around the fire with drinks in hand, Lainey – who'd gone inside to make herself a cup of tea and now stood with her arm around Brick's waist – got their attention. "Folks? We need to make an announcement."

"Yeah, so, what's going on here?" Jack Harrison said. "First you all start asking questions about our guy Ralph, and now Morgan says she's got an emergency."

For Jesse, looking at Morgan in the firelight was a little like being socked in the gut; it took his breath away. He moved closer to the fire to try to get warm, blinked and tried to focus on what she was saying: "Somebody's working for Woods and Water on the sly, stealing my recipes and then serving them up there."

In a round: "What?"; "Really?"; "Jeez!"

Morgan explained, and Jack Harrison broke in. "But the fact that they'd actually *use* your creative ideas to steal business from you – no matter who's figuring out the recipes and doing the cooking – that's just unacceptable. First things first, we'll expel them from SIBA." He glanced at Jesse and explained, "That's the Seacoast Island Business Association. We'll take them off the website and out of next year's ads. Though I guess that doesn't help you much for this year, Morgan."

"Why didn't I think of that?" Lainey said, glancing up at Brick, who shrugged and smiled down on her like she could do no wrong.

"There's always sabotage," old Caleb said, his eyes glinting. "Nothing like a well-placed stick of dynamite to make your point."

"I'll volunteer for that crew," Hannah said with a grin.

Jesse had to laugh. "I've been trying to get Morgan to see the benefits of intimidation."

"We just need to find out who the mole is and get him off the island," Morgan said. "That's where I'm relying on you. Aside from trying to steer business away from Woods and Water, too."

"I can't believe Brad could possibly be involved," Caroline Brooks said. "This is the first summer he's worked for me at the Barnacle, but he's just the sweetest boy."

"I'd trust our Paul with my life," Deborah Harrison said. "And you've already cleared Ralph, right?"

"So who's that leave?" Bev said.

"What about Uriah?" Hannah said. "I just met him the other night, but he seemed a little shifty."

"Uriah works at the Cutthroat," Morgan said, "and I don't think he does much more than burgers and sandwiches, so it's not likely he'd have the skills to figure out my recipes. That leaves the people from Brenneman's – Tom, Sam and Kevin."

"I know Tom and Sam," Hannah said. "They're pretty much into each other, have been for weeks. I can't imagine either of them would have time for this."

"Then we're left with Kevin," Morgan said.

"We'll pin him down tonight," Bev said. "Get him to admit it."

"All right, so we get Kevin to admit he's been doing this and we get him off the island," Tim Sawyer said. "But we need to go farther than that. Get the *owners* of that place off the island, too. Obviously, they're complicit. And they've been anti-social since the minute they got here and built that monstrosity." Jesse would've been surprised by the lobsterman's vocabulary, if Morgan hadn't already explained that Tim had gone to Bowdoin and was the most intelligent member of Lainey's wintertime book club. "I'm not in competition with them like you are, Morgan, but I don't like the idea of Seacoast being taken over by people like that."

"I agree," Deborah Harrison said. "We can't have people like that be part of our community."

"But their business comes solely from people who *aren't* part of our community, so it isn't like we can boycott them," Morgan said.

"Stick of dynamite, I'm telling you," Caleb suggested again.

"Ostracization can be as effective as a boycott, in the long run," Tim said.

Lainey spoke up. "We could meet tourists at the boat with flyers telling what Woods and Water's been doing, so anyone who was planning to stay there might think twice."

"We could also just go talk to them," Brick said.

"Tried that," Jesse said.

"We could picket them," Bev said.

"I like all those ideas," Morgan said, "but I still have to come up with new recipes and this judge is coming in six days. And anybody with any spare time, I'd really appreciate it if you could help Jesse on the roof."

Jesse had heard enough – and he'd been a Marine lieutenant long enough that he couldn't suppress the impulse to take command. "Listen, here's the plan. Phase one: Tonight when these squirrels show up, we gang up on 'em, especially Kevin. I'll take the lead in the interrogation. The rest of you threaten them with job loss, loss of services, kicking them off the island if they don't tell everything they know. Anything you can think of. Phase two: Tomorrow, Jack, you let the DuPages know about the SIBA decision and the reason for it. Lainey and Hannah and Bev, if you've got the time, make flyers and hand them out when the boats come in. I think for now it's best not to get right in their faces with picketing on their front porch, which they could take as a threat or trespassing." He still didn't want to mention Mrs. DuPage's lawyer. "Until they get here, let's drink and have a good time. I'll play some music. And, by the way, I'll take help on the roof, but only if you've got some experience or are a bit handy to begin with. Sound good, Morgan?"

Morgan looked partly annoyed, partly amused – and partly something he couldn't identify. "That'll do, Lieutenant Stewart."

He felt his face heat up; he grabbed his guitar.

"Grab a beer, everybody," Morgan said, like she just had to have the last word. "We'll wait for the chefs to come."

As the crowd got up and moved around, talking among themselves, Jesse sat down on the log and started strumming, feeling aggravated. Morgan ought to be glad he was here, doing his utmost to help her on every front. She didn't seem to realize he could leave any day he wanted; that it was only his sense of duty keeping him here.

Sort of, anyway.

He remembered the other night, hearing her singing in the shower. How he'd had the sense that her voice was just aching to be heard; and how much he wanted to hear it.

No time like the present, it seemed, especially since he was going to be leaving this place as soon as he possibly could – after his gig on Friday, anyway. He needed to get back home and away from these feelings that Morgan was stirring up in him – feelings that, because of who she was, had no chance of leading to anything but upset. He hadn't talked to Tammy again, but she'd sent a few restive texts, and if he had any prayer of making anything of what he had with her, it'd have to be soon. Plus, his dad had called, saying he'd just won a huge bid and wanting to know when Jesse was going to be back at work.

"Hey," Jesse said to the crowd, "did you all know Morgan used to be the lead singer in a band?"

That got their attention. "Really?" someone said, and another said, "No kidding!"

Morgan glared like she'd as soon kill him.

Jesse grinned. "And since I've got a song in mind that requires two voices, I think she oughto sing this one with me. What do you all think?"

"Wonderful idea!" Lainey said.

"Go, Morgan!" Hannah said. Others backed the sentiment.

"I don't think so," Morgan said.

"Aw, come on, Morgan," Jesse said. "What's it gonna hurt?"

12

With Jesse shooting her his most charming grin and everybody else egging her on, Morgan felt like her worst fear was coming true. She hadn't sung in front of an audience in six years. She'd barely even sung in the shower.

"I couldn't," she said.

"Give an old man a thrill," Caleb Brown said.

Jesse switched chords, not taking his enticing eyes off her, and in a few seconds she recognized "Whenever You Come Around."

Oh, she loved this song. Her band had performed it countless times, her guitar player singing the harmonies on the chorus, Vince Gill's part to Morgan's Alison Krauss.

"Morgan, Morgan," Hannah started chanting softly, and others joined in.

"Come on over," Jesse told her, with a sweeping nod of his head, in a tone meant for the whole crowd, as if it were a foregone conclusion that she would follow his command. Bad enough he'd started issuing everybody orders about Woods and Water! Not that he'd had bad ideas; just the principle annoyed her. And it was so obnoxious how he so clearly believed that by smiling that way at somebody – at *her* – he'd get whatever he wanted.

Never mind that he looked so good that he actually *could* make her ready to do things she'd never dream of normally.

She realized: he was actually making her question the whole way she'd been living her life. She knew she'd been in mourning when she'd arrived here – she'd wanted to focus on making the B&B a success, on meeting other people's needs, on keeping herself so busy she didn't have time to be sad. She'd wanted to deaden all her senses, so she wouldn't be stricken down with pain.

But she'd been doing that for six years. If she wasn't careful, was it going to become the permanent state of the rest of her life? Like parents said to children, "Your face might freeze that way." Was *she* frozen?

Looking at Jesse, she thought she didn't *want* to be. This was the first time she'd ever thought that, and that scared her.

Lainey came up to Morgan's elbow. "How come you never told me you sang?"

"It was such a long time ago," Morgan said. Jesse hadn't taken his eyes off her. He was just playing the opening chords over and over again, waiting. He mouthed, *Come on,* looking to her like the devil who would promise that if you walked across *this* fire you wouldn't get burned.

Lainey nudged her. "Oh, go on, it'll be fun." The light in her eyes said she just couldn't wait to see Morgan go sit beside Jesse, as if that could prove what she'd been saying about sparks flying between them. "Besides, this crowd isn't going to let you off the hook. And you're among friends here."

Morgan looked around, realized that was true, and gave up resisting. Here was her chance to brave unlocking a part of herself that she'd kept stashed behind closed doors all this time. Like Lainey said, this was a safe place to do that. And the way Jesse was looking at her made her *want* to be brave, somehow – even if he might also seem like a devil, doing it.

Besides, it was a perfect chance to prove to Lainey – and herself – that there was nothing between her and Jesse except friendship.

She made her way around the fire. People moved to make room, and she sat next to him on the log. He gave her that smile that showcased his dimples. She was too nervous to smile back, but, when the moment came, she started to sing.

She hadn't sung for anyone in years, but she saw people start to smile.

Encouraged, she took a breath and kept going, glancing at Jesse, who was watching her with soft eyes.

Morgan's heart thunked in response, and, suddenly, everything started to take on new meaning. *Oh, no,* she thought, as she sang the lines about not being able to find words, because those lines felt true, and, when Jesse came in on the chorus, his voice harmonizing with hers about weak knees and breathlessness, she all but lost her breath herself. She struggled to keep her voice under control. And when she sang about a smile that turned the world on its head, he was smiling at her that way for real, and how was she going to sing the second verse?

Somehow, she did. Keeping her feelings hidden, just like in the song. But his voice blending with hers gave her such powerful chills that she wondered how she could have thought that her attraction to him was merely physical, and she didn't know what she would possibly do with the knowledge that it was more.

During the instrumental verse, while he played the melody on the guitar, she watched his hands, and then she sang the chorus again, harmonizing with him, and nothing had ever sounded so wonderful to her ears. His voice snaked through her body, and when their voices blended, parts of her were letting go of old regrets and soaring with joy at how it felt to find her voice again – and to hear how perfectly it could blend with another human being's.

Another man's.

Her husband's best friend.

She didn't even wait for the applause to die down before she jumped up and ran inside the house. In the bathroom, she splashed cold water on her face and patted it dry. She looked in her own green eyes in the mirror. "Jesse Stewart? Get a hold of yourself," she said out loud, and she went out to the kitchen and made herself busy hunting through her cupboards for graham crackers and chocolate. People might want S'mores, for God's sake! Where had her brain been, these last few days? And where was it right now? She usually knew the locations of everything in her cupboards, but now she just could not seem to think straight.

And what on earth had she been thinking that exposing herself – singing again, letting herself feel things – could be a good idea? Better to keep everything locked inside – frozen – like her original idea of six years ago. Otherwise, she chanced breaking down completely.

And she couldn't risk opening her heart up to Jesse, of all people. Even if he *hadn't* been Rick's best friend, he was a man with the word 'disaster' written all over him. A man with a track record like his, and with an established life – not to mention a girlfriend – a thousand miles away.

She had to stop letting herself be so drawn to him. She just had to. It was bad enough that Rick was feeling farther and farther away, these last few days.

"Hey," came a voice behind her. Jesse.

13

"You doing all right?" Jesse asked, though it was obvious that Morgan *wasn't*, the manic way she'd gone right back to rifling through the cupboards after turning to freeze him with a look. He just didn't know what else to say.

"Come on, it wasn't that bad," he said, laughing a little. "I thought we sounded pretty good, actually." Of course, he'd thought – and felt – far more than that. Just as he'd suspected, her voice blending with his had completely enchanted him. His mom would say playing with fire that way – insisting Morgan sing with him – was "just like" him. And now he'd opened the door to more feelings of the type he'd been avoiding the last several days, and of the very type he'd just been telling himself could lead to nothing but upset.

But the desire and attraction he felt for Morgan right now was dazzling him in a way he'd never been dazzled, and he found it impossible not to want to push it farther, to feel more. The thrill and fear of it was like standing on a high bridge getting ready to make a bungee jump, hoping the harness would hold.

"Everybody said so," he went on, "if you'd've stuck around long enough to hear them."

"You had no right to ask me to sing like that," she said, still rummaging through cupboards. "In front of everybody."

"What are you looking for?"

She turned to him, her eyes on fire. "Chocolate! Graham crackers! Why didn't we ever think that people might want S'mores?" She went back to the cupboards.

Jesse didn't want her to shut him out any more that way, that same way she'd been doing every time they'd gotten a little closer these last few days. And there were times *he'd* been the one to shut *her* out, and he didn't want to keep doing that, either. There was honor and being faithful to someone's memory – and then there was plum foolishness, turning away from something that just might be the very thing that would put the stars back in your eyes. "Why don't you stop taking care of everybody else for two seconds," he said, "and start thinking about what *you* need?"

She came up with chocolate bars and a box of graham crackers. She closed the cupboard door and fixed him in her hot gaze again. "And you think you have some idea what that is?"

"I didn't say that. I'm saying maybe you should start asking yourself."

The auburn streaks in her hair glowed in the kitchen light. She blinked. "Stop looking at me like that."

Relieved to think she might be nervous, too, he felt powerless but to want to see what could happen. He took one step closer, reached out and took the cracker box from her, then the chocolate. He set them on the counter. She was watching him with wide eyes, not moving. He put his hands on her waist. "What's that gonna solve?" he said, and the curves of her mouth were fascinating him again.

"Jesse," she said, and, as he inched closer, breathing the sweet lavender scent of her hair, she put her hands on his chest, and not exactly to push him away.

It would've been typical for him make some smartass comment to deflect any genuine feeling that might be roiling up, then lean in for the kiss. Morgan made him want to be different. Better. Real.

"I think you miss singing," he said.

She opened her mouth to speak. Just then, from the edge of the room, came a man's nasally voice. "Morgan, my wife and I can't make heads nor tails of this ferry schedule." A bald man was just entering from the guest portion of the house, not looking up from the brochure he was reading. Morgan took four quick steps back from Jesse, eyes wide like she'd been caught doing something illegal. Left alone, he was wrought up, hollow. The man went on, oblivious. "Would you tell us how we're supposed to time everything with checking out and getting our luggage down to the dock?"

"Mr. Bridges!" Morgan said. "Of course, I'll explain everything. Say, I don't think I saw you this afternoon to tell you that we're having a campfire outside. You're welcome to join us for S'mores."

"Oh, is that what that music was?" Mr. Bridges sniffed. "My wife hopes it won't go very late. She requires a certain amount of beauty sleep."

"Of course," Morgan assured him, picking up the graham crackers and chocolate from the counter. She handed them to Jesse, whose expectations for the evening were undergoing a massive degree of downshifting. "Jesse," she said, "would you take these outside and tell everyone we're adjourning after two more songs? You don't mind playing a couple more, do you?"

"No, I don't, but what about…?" He meant confronting Kevin and the other chefs – a task which admittedly had slid to the back of his mind ever since they'd sung together and he'd followed her into the kitchen.

"We can see who's here in a few minutes and go from there." Morgan turned to take the brochure from her guest. "Now, Mr. Bridges, let me see what we have here."

Jesse decided the best thing to do was show some patience. The old dude's cluelessness was aggravating, but Jesse couldn't very well shove the guy out of the kitchen – not if he wanted to stay on Morgan's good side.

Which he definitely did.

There were a lot of hours left in this night. He took the crackers and chocolate outside, knowing she'd be following soon.

But when she came out and he asked her to sing again, she refused, despite the urging of the crowd, and wouldn't meet his eyes. By the time the evening had wrapped up, not too long later – with Kevin continuing to insist he had no idea about the recipes, and Tom and Sam and Uriah no-shows – Morgan *still* wouldn't look at Jesse, and she busied herself cleaning up around the fire, dousing it with a bucket of water into a flat steaming pile. Jesse, who'd been hoping to sit out next to it with her and only her and look at the stars, settled for following her inside carrying his guitar and a carton of empties, while she brought in what little remained of the S'mores supplies.

"I thought sure he'd admit it to me," he said, remembering the frightened look in Kevin's eyes when Jesse'd gotten in his little weasel face to inform him that, by process of elimination, they'd decided he was guilty. "But I could hardly start pounding on him. Unfortunately, I think he was telling the truth."

Morgan laughed a little. "No, pounding on him wouldn't have been good." She set the cracker box on the counter and started pulling out empty wrappers, shoving them into the trash can under the sink. "So, if he's telling the truth, then our theory's blown and we're back to square one."

Her acting so distant made his heart actually hurt. He put down what he was carrying and went up behind her, touching the small of her back so she'd turn to face him. "Morgan, talk to me. That wasn't nothing, earlier. You can't tell me it was."

She swallowed. Folded her arms, turned so he couldn't keep his hand on her back, and leaned against the counter. Her eyes were deep, and he couldn't tell if she was sad or something else. "What I think is three things," she said. She blinked and folded her arms tighter, as if trying to keep herself from touching him – though maybe he was dreaming about that. "One is, you're my friend, and you were Rick's friend, and you're the only connection I have left with him. Two, you're planning to leave on Saturday, and today's Wednesday already. Three, you have a girlfriend and a job waiting for you back in North Carolina, a thousand miles away."

Hard facts, and all so bruising that he didn't want to admit they were true. "You didn't feel something?"

She frowned, an actual frown that turned down the corners of her mouth and puckered the skin between her eyebrows. "Whatever I felt or didn't feel in that one moment when I was upset about singing again has got to be overruled by those three things." She nodded, underscoring the point. "That's what I think."

He leaned back against the island, across from her. He didn't want to be mad, but he was a whole mess of things. His head knew she was right about the facts, but his heart was screaming something else.

"Besides," she went on, "who knows what's really *real*, in a case like this? You're here, I'm here, you look so good, and I've been alone so long."

That was a slap in the face. "You don't think what's going on here is anything real?"

She looked at the ceiling. "It's just that I don't *know*. What if it's just, you know, an interlude? Between real life and real life? Besides, I know your track record. Your outlook. The way you always make sure to disappoint someone before they can disappoint you first."

He winced at that. "Believe it or not, I would never want to disappoint you," he said, because it was one thing that was true, one thing he was thinking, even as he couldn't completely identify all of what he was feeling.

Her eyes glistened as she looked at him. Then, still with her arms folded, she took two steps toward him and pressed her forehead to his chest, and his pounding heart itself yearned to reach for her. He made himself stand still, and it wasn't long before his chance to try to change her mind was past. She straightened. "Jesse."

Wanting to lean down and kiss her, he touched his finger to her soft lips instead. He couldn't help not wanting to let the door shut entirely, though. "It *is* confusing," he said. "For me, too."

"Do you have to go?" She said it like a sudden inspiration, and her eyes brightened. "On Saturday, do you have to go?"

His heart sped up.

"I mean, you can certainly keep working on the roof until Monday, if you don't mind. I don't get *that* many walk-ins over the weekend. But, even after the judge gets here, you can stay. Take a few days off. Help me entertain her. After the weekend, you can have one of the guest rooms, if you want. Stay and relax, maybe set up another gig at the Barnacle. Let me cook for you. It would be the least I could do, after everything you've done for me."

"Now *I'm* confused," he said, and he laughed because that was all he could think to do. "But I *could* use more time on the roof." Though that was about the lowest thing on the list of things he cared about right this second.

"I like having you around," she said simply. "I know you have to go back to Fayetteville soon, but why does it have to be Saturday? Stay as my friend, who knows I need a little more help getting ready for winter. Stay because you like it here."

"It's *cold* here," he said, smiling.

She laughed. "Whatever. Wimp."

"Morgan Bailey," he said, because he really wanted to kiss her right then, she was so knock-your-socks-off gorgeous, and he didn't know that staying a few extra days wouldn't seem like torture, trying to keep his distance from her at the same time he was feeling so drawn to her – and so uncertain about what *she* felt about him.

"What if I said I needed you?" she said. "That garden, you know? And we still don't know who the mole is or how Woods and Water's getting hold of my recipes. And how am I going to keep my sanity, with all of that going on and then entertaining this judge, to boot? If you stayed, you could make her feel welcome with your Southern charm, maybe show her around the island and things, while I'm going crazy in the kitchen. You know, almost nobody who runs a B&B does it by themselves. It usually takes two."

"I *can* see it's too much work for any one sane person."

"Yes, it is." She was looking at him with those big green eyes, and there was no way he could say no, or say he didn't want to spend more time with her, even if it might not lead to anything, even if she said it couldn't.

A few more days, though? That would be heaven – or hell, one of the two.

"Let me think on it overnight," he said.

"Good!" She stood on tiptoe and kissed his cheek, and the impact of her soft lips made him close his eyes for a second. When he opened them, she was gone, and he heard the French doors open and shut, leaving him more confused than ever.

Was she right that the plum foolishness part of this situation would be to try for something that, according to the facts as she laid them out, had no chance in hell of turning out well? Something that *she* said might be nothing more than an "interlude," something not even "real." Was she right that trying for more might be like making a big jump off a bridge with no harness at all, maybe just a rope that your hands for sure wouldn't be able to grip for long? Thrilling on the way down, sure – but you'd wind up hurt or dead for your trouble.

So why did she want him to stay?

To check in with the life he had – his "real" life, he guessed Morgan would say – he called Tammy. She actually answered. "Jesse?"

"Hey, stranger," he said, making his voice sound like nothing else in the world but her was on his mind.

"You've got that right, stranger," she snapped. "I hope you're calling to tell me you're on your way back home."

Whatever optimism he might've had popped like a balloon. "No," he said, drawing out the word into about three syllables, his old smartass self coming right back to the surface.

"Jesse! It's been two weeks since I've seen you. I don't know how much longer I can hold off all these guys at the dance hall."

He sighed. He thought about how he'd felt a few moments ago, standing in the kitchen with Morgan. Perfectly content, totally engaged – and like there was nowhere else he'd rather be in the world.

Then he remembered how he'd felt the times he'd spent with Tammy. In retrospect, he saw he'd just been biding his time. Hoping something better might come along, without actually believing it could.

That wasn't enough, he realized. His "real" life had to be more.

He remembered how, when he was a kid, he'd always said he wanted to grow up to be just like his grandpa: A hard-working farmer who could fix anything and seemed to know everything.

But the truly important part of his grandpa's life that Jesse had recognized as a child was the way Grandpa looked at Jesse's grandma like she hung the moon, and how she'd looked at him the same, and how neither ever had an unkind word to say about the other, and how every day they made each other laugh.

Then there was the way Grandpa's five kids relied on him, looked up to him, and knew he'd be there for them come hell or high water. There was the wild swirl of activity that came with a big family – five kids, eleven grandkids, and none of them lived far away, so the cousins were always running in and out and around, and on holidays everybody was there for sure.

But no matter how wild the days were, each one ended with a peaceful good night kiss for everyone from Grandpa and Grandma.

Yeah, knowing how to do things and fix things was great, but that *feeling*, Jesse realized, that was what he'd actually wanted to recreate in his own life. Family. Love. Heaps and heaps of it.

How could he have lost sight of *that* dream, all these years?

He knew, though. When his mom had walked out on his dad when Jesse was only fourteen, with no particular warning and her only explanation that she wanted to "contribute something to the world" (though she still "loved" Jesse's dad "but just not quite *enough*"), Jesse'd turned cynical. Maybe he'd even decided, deep down, without exactly realizing it, in a sullen teenaged way, that love like his grandparents' just didn't *exist* these days.

And what had happened with Dawn – and all the other women he'd crossed paths with since – only confirmed that.

But now he knew he had to take a chance it *might*.

Clearly, he wasn't going to find any such thing with Tammy – or anyone else who made him feel that he'd just as soon be washing his truck as having a conversation with her. "Tell you what," he told her. "Why don't you *stop* trying to hold those fellas off?"

A shocked pause. "What do you mean?"

"I mean let's forget this. You go on and see what somebody else has to offer you. 'Cause it's clear I'm not offering you *enough*."

"Jesse, I didn't mean… I'm just dying to see you, that's all."

"Bye, Tammy," he said, and when he hung up he felt he'd set himself free.

And instantly he decided: He'd call his dad tomorrow. His dad – and Buster, too – would just have to understand: Jesse needed a few more days away.

14

Friday night at the Barnacle, which was still crowded long past the dinner hour, Morgan watched as Jesse made his way up onto the tiny stage to play, and she couldn't help grinning when he winked at her. He just looked so damn good, wearing his customary straw cowboy hat, a flannel shirt, jeans and his "purely for style" cowboy boots. As he sat down on the stool provided, adjusted the microphone, and began tuning his guitar, Lainey leaned close to Morgan. "Are you sure you told me *everything* that happened the other night?"

"Yes, I did." Morgan had filled Lainey in about that moment in the kitchen on Wednesday when Mr. Bridges had, fortunately, interrupted her and Jesse before she could let her feelings run away with her; before anything really stupid could happen, in other words. "And let's talk about you two for a moment," she said, including Brick, who was sitting on Lainey's other side. "Inquiring minds want to know. Are you pregnant or not? You *must* know by now."

Brick smiled secretively, but Lainey ignored the questions completely. "I can't believe you told Jesse that this was an 'interlude,'" she said, shaking her head.

"The way you two sang together. Boy, that was something to behold."

"I think *he* might be considering it as something more," Brick said. "From the way he talks about you."

Morgan's face heated up. What had Jesse *said* to Brick? She couldn't bear to know. "Well, it *is* an interlude. He's here for only a short time."

Brick held up his hands. "Just sayin'. Anybody need anything from the bar?" They shook their heads, and he got up and headed over there.

Lainey wasn't finished. "Listen, when you asked Jesse to stay a few extra days, he didn't blink, right?"

"He had to think about it overnight."

Lainey rolled her eyes, as Hannah came over and pulled up a chair. "What did I miss?"

"We were just talking about Jesse and Morgan."

Hannah grinned. "You sleep with him yet?"

Morgan heart banged. "What?" It seemed like sacrilege to mention such an outlandish possibility so casually.

Hannah shrugged. "Everyone sees the way you look at each other. Why don't you take a chance? See what happens? Maybe you'd get him out of your system."

"That's right," Lainey said. "Otherwise you're always going to be wondering 'what if.' Besides, how often does anyone get to experience the way you two smile at each other? Especially out here?"

Morgan's face was hot. Get him out of her system? Could that work? Did she even *want* to? "He's my main connection to Rick. I want to keep him as a friend."

Hannah grinned. "You do not. You want to take him to bed. It's written all over your face."

Lainey leaned close and whispered, "If things work out, maybe he'd think about staying for good."

"That's ridiculous."

Hannah shook her head. "I think the two of you have gotten *way* past the 'he was my husband's best friend' stage. I mean, look at the way he's stepped up to the plate about this whole Woods and Water thing. A guy doesn't do all that just out of being 'friends.' He doesn't do all that unless he's *interested*."

Jesse had helped Morgan, Lainey, Brick, Hannah, and Bev fold anti-Woods and Water flyers late into the night last night, and early this morning he'd brought them to the post office, paid out of his own pocket for them to be stuck in all hundred and eighteen boxes, then went around posting the extras on bulletin boards all over town. He'd also treated each of the chefs to a private interrogation, Marine style, though they all still claimed to know nothing. Then Jack Harrison said that Mrs. DuPage had refused to acknowledge that she was doing anything less than above board, and had threatened legal action if the "intimidation tactics" didn't cease. Mr. DuPage, Jack said, still hadn't shown his face.

At that point, Morgan had told everyone that for the next few days she needed to focus on getting ready for the judge's arrival; that the mole had done all the damage he was going to as far as the contest was concerned, since the tasting group was no longer meeting. Besides, most of the chefs would leave the island when the restaurants closed for the season, so if Woods and Water kept serving spectacular breakfasts, who was doing the cooking would be made clear by the sheer fact of who was left.

For now, Morgan had to focus on the major problem of having no idea what she was going to cook for Ally.

Though, for a major problem, it was taking up an unreasonably small portion of her brain. She was trying to come up with ideas, but, given all that was at stake, she wasn't as *worried* as she really should have been. Meanwhile, Jesse was taking up the rest. His voice. His smile. The warmth of his hands on her waist, those couple of times. The way he looked sleeping when she walked past him in the mornings...

She shook her head. "He's here helping me because of Rick, remember? Not because he's 'interested.' Anyway, Lainey, not everybody can be like you and Brick. Not every man is willing to give up his life and move to an island. Even to start to *dream* that Jesse could be would be unrealistic. Because that's all it would ever be – a dream. And I'd lose him as a friend and my heart would get battered to pieces along the way. Besides, we don't even have anything in common!"

"See, you're thinking about it."

"I am not." A lie, of course, and Lainey's grin said she knew it.

Brick returned with a fresh beer for himself and sparkling water for Lainey.

"Ah ha," Hannah said.

"You have to tell me!" Morgan said.

"Shh," Lainey said with a tiny grin, as, up on stage, Jesse said, "Thanks, everyone, for being here. I'd like to start out with a little song I wrote a long time ago." He started playing the chords, and Morgan was reminded of the past again. Jesse's songs often had the feel and sound of songs from the late '90s, the years when she'd been singing her heart out and dreaming of making it big. Before she'd met Rick; before she'd found new dreams with him then lost them.

She wondered if Jesse knew all that – if he was trying to remind her that she'd had this whole other set of dreams once, back before she'd even known Rick was in the world.

He began to sing: "Back home, are you missing me? Back home, that's where I want to be…"

His voice sent chills and warmth at once coursing through her, and she blinked back tears, remembering what it had been like to be the girl who was waiting back home.

"Dear Mom, thanks for the cookies. Dear Dad, I'm doin' my duty. But that don't mean I'm not dreamin' of the time… we went swimmin' at the pond after school, waited on the girls down at the pool, drove our pickup trucks out to the lake; we went runnin' 'round Grandpa's farm, stayin' just one breath from harm, found a way to cure most mistakes…"

Her heart swelling with feeling for him, Morgan tried not to think about what Lainey had just said about a guy not going out of his way the way Jesse had unless he was interested – or about how intoxicating it had been to hear his voice blending with hers, and to be close to him that night in the kitchen, with him moving closer...

She was glad Mr. Bridges had broken in, but it was hard not to wonder what might have happened if he hadn't. She had a feeling it could have been something amazing. Scary as hell, but amazing.

"Dear Jake," Jesse sang, "Stay in school. Dear Ray, Marines rule. But that don't mean I'm not dreamin' of the time…"

And if it would have been amazing then, it might actually be even more amazing now. The last couple of days, she and Jesse had been pretending they were simply the best of friends, like there wasn't and never could be any chemistry between them. And, since they were getting along so well and talking about everything under the sun, she was only growing to like him more.

Now, as his voice soared on the chorus, she wiped away another tear, remembering the stories he'd been telling her about his time in Iraq and Afghanistan, including some funny ones that featured Rick. For the first time, she'd found herself being happy at the memory of Rick, instead of sad. Her heart had melted at Jesse's telling of how they'd adopted Buster over there, and all the trouble Jesse'd gone to to get the dog home to North Carolina. Her heart had melted a little more when he told about his grandparents and their farm, holidays with all his aunts and uncles and cousins, his disappointment that he and his brother couldn't seem to get along for five minutes – and a little more still when he talked about how much he admired his dad and loved his mom; how much it had meant to him that his mom had kept in close touch the whole time he was overseas; how he was still struggling to forgive her, all these years later, for breaking up their family. He said that being out of the Marines ("and being *here*, to be honest with you") was giving him clarity about what he wanted out of life, though he was vague about what that was. He said he hadn't totally given up the "pipe dream" of going to Nashville, that in "weaker moments" he still wanted to see if he could make it as a professional musician.

Morgan, in turn, had confessed how it wasn't just Rick's family she'd been distant from since his death; that her own parents wondered why they rarely heard from her; that she'd seen her niece and nephew, who were seven and five and lived in New Hampshire near her parents, only twice in their lives. Jesse listened intently, apparently without judgment, saying only, "It may be time to stop letting life pass you by that way. Family's the most important thing there is."

The song he was singing right now showed he actually believed that through and through. And he sounded so good that she couldn't help believing that his dream of making it in Nashville wasn't a pipe dream at all.

Meanwhile, he'd worked about as hard on the roof and garden as she'd ever seen anyone work, and she couldn't help admiring the qualities that led him to do that: his loyalty, his work ethic, his sense of honor and duty. She kept finding herself touching his arm, his back, whenever he was in her path; and, whenever he walked by her, he'd give her a friendly nudge on the arm, or, when they were sitting side by side, rest his hand briefly on her knee. She'd try to ignore the way her blood heated at his touch, and tell herself all the same reasons why not, in a kind of refrain.

Why did he have to be so admirable, anyway? Sometimes she wished she hadn't asked him to stay longer, because the pain of parting with him was bound to be bad – but she really did need his help. And, despite herself, she really didn't want to rush him out. She hated to think of the day when she'd wake up without him in the next room; the night when she'd eat supper alone.

Now, he sang the chorus one last time and played the final chords, singing softly, "Yeah, I'm missing you all. I'm... missing... you."

The crowd burst into applause. Morgan, cheering, too, felt proud to be the reason he was on the island. He modestly tugged his hat brim and gave a cute little smile, then went right back to playing fresh chords. The crowd quickly quieted to hear him. "Thanks, folks. Here's a little song I wrote more recently." Morgan felt his eyes lock with hers, and she felt her face heat up. He looked down at his hands again, his bowed head hidden under his hat, then looked up and sang. "Lyin' here all night, lookin' at the ceiling, hearin' you breathe not far away...."

She froze. Could this be about *her*? No way.

But she listened, rapt, as his voice soared on lines about unrequited love, about dreaming and scheming that things could be different, about savoring the memory of a so-called accidental touch. Her face got hot, as she thought of the times in the last few days when she'd made excuses to brush past him in the kitchen, to touch his back or his arm, and she hoped in the dim light he couldn't see her blushing.

Am I being an idiot? she thought. *Are Lainey and Hannah right?* Clearly, she was feeling things for Jesse she hadn't felt in practically a lifetime.

But it still seemed wrong to cross that line with Rick's best friend. Besides, Jesse was leaving. Leaving. And surely this song wasn't about her.

Jesse played the last chord, and the crowd whooped and hollered. Morgan clapped so hard her hands hurt. Lainey leaned over again. "Morgan, for Pete's sake, he clearly wrote that for you. He's *pining* for you."

"No way," Morgan said, and, when Jesse met her eyes from up on the stage, she smiled like she was his best friend and had no idea that anything else could ever cross either of their minds.

Heading home, Morgan and Jesse walked ahead, while Lainey and Brick trailed behind. Hannah had gone off in the opposite direction, toward her family's huge summer cottage, which would be shut down for the season when she went back to New York.

"Now all we have to do is get *you* up on stage," Jesse told Morgan, his voice warm in the darkness. The stars were out and the night was crisp. "Karaoke tomorrow? What do you say?"

Morgan folded her arms, wanting to know – and terrified to know – if he'd written that song since he'd been here. "Tomorrow? Are you kidding? I have *got* to figure out what I'm going to cook for Ally. Besides, I can't be leaving my guests to their own devices all the time. Bad enough I left them tonight."

"They're grown-ups. Anyway, you'll figure something out for Ally. Like I told you, you have to let your unconscious mind work on the problem, while you go out and have some fun. Like tonight."

She laughed. "You have more confidence than I do."

He nudged her slightly, and she felt a shudder down to her toes, and they walked in amiable silence the rest of the way. When they got to the B&B and bid Lainey and Brick goodnight, Jesse went to put his guitar case away, and Morgan went into the kitchen. She didn't think he'd follow, so when he came in as she was measuring out coffee for the morning, she was startled, and happy, and when he smiled, her heart sped up. She tried to slow it down, to remember about just being friends, all the things she'd told Lainey – and herself. She tried not to think of the words of that song he'd sung. "You were really good tonight," she said.

The praise made him grin like a teenager. "Thanks. Thanks for setting it up for me."

"You're welcome."

He stretched his arms above his head, a nonchalant gesture that meant nothing, and when his shirt lifted up, revealing his abs and his belt buckle, she had to look away.

"What did you think of my new song?" he said.

"It was great!" she said, staying busy.

A long pause. "So, karaoke tomorrow?"

She laughed and looked at him again. "Mr. Persistence."

He grinned.

She shook her head, smiling. "Honestly, Jesse, help me think. What am I going to cook for Ally? I've *got* to figure it out, like, tonight, so I can order any special ingredients I need."

His brow wrinkled with concern. "I hadn't thought of that."

"'Simple food. What the hell *is* that, even? I guess I've been making everything pretty complicated for a long time."

"Well, let me think. My grandma used to make us biscuits and gravy. How about that? You couldn't get much simpler than that, right?"

"I can't make a Southern dish to represent the New England division."

"All right, then. Seems to me someone wrote a New England breakfast cookbook some time back." He went to the shelf and pulled down her old volume.

"How did you even know about that?"

"Snooping." He grinned, and, wow, Lainey was right, everything inside her did a backflip.

He started paging through the volume. "How about your so-called old standby, blueberry pancakes?"

"Those recipes are all four or five years old. My culinary skills are way advanced from then."

"Maybe, but Lainey was telling me this book's still her biggest seller. And it put this place on the map, right? Got that editor to seek you out?"

"All right, but, even so, I can't just take recipes directly from that book. They have to be fresh ideas."

"Fine, but going back to basics is never a bad idea, right?" He looked up and grinned again. "Says so right here. 'Chapter One: Back to Basics.' You talk about using what you have locally. Lobster and things like that."

"Let me see that." Her mind was already spinning in new directions as he handed it over. "I got so sick of cooking and picking lobster that I stopped a couple years ago. Besides, tourists usually eat it for lunch or dinner, and most don't want it three meals a day."

"But, for your contest, it might be just the thing to represent the region."

Knowing he was right, she didn't look up from words she'd written a long time ago and since forgotten. *The key to any great breakfast is simplicity... A few quality, fresh, local ingredients go a long way... Don't overwhelm your guests with too many flavors – they haven't been awake for long, remember!*

She could get the freshest possible lobster from Tim Sawyer. She still had apples on the tree in her yard, a few blueberries lingering on the bushes, arugula and corn and tomatoes and herbs still hanging on in the garden. Surely she could get laid-that-morning eggs from Bev Hargrove if she paid top dollar for the best ones to be reserved. Extremely fresh, basic ingredients – that was the key to simple food.

"I'll leave you to your creating," Jesse said. "But call me if you need me, all right? I'll just be in the next room."

"Great, thanks," she said, flipping to the seafood chapter.

Time passed in a blur, as her old ideas inspired new ones, and by the time she'd decided what she would make for all three contest entries, she was surprised to see the clock: nearly two a.m. She had to be up in three hours to make breakfast – it would have to be blueberry pancakes again. To be safe, she wasn't going to share her new ideas with – or cook them for – anyone except Jesse.

She shoved her notes into the drawer and shut out the lights, eager to see him and tell him what she'd come up with, though of course when she went into the living room, he was asleep – on the couch with his clothes and the TV on, like maybe he'd been trying to wait up for her.

His face looked so sweet and handsome while he was sleeping. For a moment, she thought of waking him to thank him for pointing her in the right direction.

But it was two a.m. Still, half hoping he *would* wake up, she clicked off the TV and the light. He didn't stir – not even when she spread a blanket over the length of his body. She watched him a moment, wondering what would happen if she touched his face – or kissed his beautiful mouth. Would he wake up? Think he was dreaming? Grab her and pull her down…?

She shook her head clear and went to her bedroom alone.

15

"So, how's that girl back home? Still texting you?" Morgan said the next night, Saturday, not looking at Jesse as they walked toward town, toward the Cutthroat and karaoke night.

Jesse'd been working on the roof all day and had gotten enough finished to feel good about it, and had worked hard enough he was sore. He'd tasted two of Morgan's new recipes – "apple-rosemary crepes with crème brulée sauce" and "lobster on toast with arugula, corn, poached eggs and savory sauce" as she called them; he was trying to convince her to give them catchier names – this afternoon when she'd practiced them, and he'd managed to convince her that not only were they perfect on the first go-round but that she owed him a karaoke duet in exchange for his inspiring her. He'd even talked all her guests into going to the Cutthroat, too, so she couldn't use needing to take care of them as an excuse to stay home.

Thing was, he'd loved singing at the Barnacle last night. The adoration of the crowd hadn't been hard to take, plus Caroline Brooks had begged him to come back and perform again. Best of all, he'd taken his chances expressing himself to Morgan in a song and at least hadn't crashed and burned. He'd told Caroline he'd play again on Wednesday, because he wanted to be available to help Morgan any way she needed with getting ready for that judge.

In the meantime, he was determined to keep breaking Morgan out of her shell, and to hear her voice blend with his again. If it had to be karaoke, that was a start.

His efforts were already paying off. She'd come out of her bedroom wearing a flared black skirt and fitted jacket with a green silk camisole peeking through, plus lip gloss, a thin necklace with a green stone pendant, and ballet flats in place of her usual Wellies. "Whoa!" he'd blurted, as his eyes roved from the bare skin highlighted by that necklace all the way down to her bare legs. The whole picture of her was about as enticing as he could stand, and seemed to only be made more so by having been kept hidden for so long. She'd blushed and said, "Aw," but seemed pleased, and added under her breath how she never usually went out at night; how she never had any excuse to dress up; how these were just old clothes she hadn't worn in years; how she might've worn heels if there wasn't a chance of killing herself walking on the gravel road. "Morgan, hush," he'd told her. "You look wonderful." And she'd smiled and laughed and tossed her hair like she was poking fun at her efforts – a gesture that had only made her *more* enticing, when he wouldn't have thought that possible.

Now she was walking with her arms folded, and he worried she might be cold. (God knew *he* was, but that was nothing new.) Usually, he would've used that as a good excuse to slip his arm around a girl, but this time he didn't, and he suddenly realized how much was at stake for him, how he didn't want to make one wrong move. In fact, he was hoping to figure out a right one. She'd been nothing but friendly the last few days, ever since she'd told him in the kitchen Wednesday night all her reasons why nothing could happen between them, and even last night, when most girls, in his experience, might've fallen for his singing. Still, he hadn't been able to turn down his attraction to her – in fact, the more time they spent together, the more intense his feelings got.

And he was past the point of actually wanting to leave to get away from those feelings. Despite what she'd said the other night, he wanted to see where they might take him. He had a suspicion that with her he might actually be able to find that old dream of love and family he was looking for, if only she'd let down her guard.

As for Rick, Jesse had decided he was pretty sure that Rick would've understood. He thought, if the tables had been turned, he himself would've wanted people he cared about to find happiness – in whatever way they could.

His dad, understanding when Jesse had explained his need to stay gone longer, had said something similar, and said he was glad Jesse was taking a chance on love, and that what had happened between him and Jesse's mom had been the result of two people who loved each other forgetting to pay attention as the years passed by. "Remember, son, you're playing the long game with this one," he'd said. (Years back, he'd volunteered to coach Jesse's PeeWee football games, and, ever since, he'd used football metaphors at every opportunity.) Then he'd mentioned that the weather would be closing in on Fayetteville soon, and that he'd promised to have this huge job done before it did, so Jesse needed to get back home as soon as possible. "Besides, Buster needs you. Whines a lot." Jesse wasn't sure how all that was supposed to work with the "long game," but whatever.

"Nope, she gave up texting me," he told Morgan now, and his nerves kicked in. This would be the first time he'd mentioned that he no longer had that particular tie to home, and he didn't know how Morgan would feel about it. Last night, even after he'd sung that song for her, she'd seemed to have nothing more than her recipes on her mind, so he'd given her her space, trying to understand, secretly hoping she'd come find him for his opinions, moral support – something. Instead, he'd fallen asleep with the TV on and woken up this morning with it off, covered by a blanket he knew he hadn't covered *himself* with, and wished he hadn't slept through her being near.

"Why?" she said. "Did you actually get her to talk to you?"

He laughed, trying to act cool. "No, she made it clear that if I was going to stay gone this long, she had other options. I told her to go with God."

"Seriously? You left another one in your dust?"

"Now, come on. It wasn't like *that*."

"I see. Were her expectations getting too high for you?"

"For God's sake. I'm here helping you, and she didn't like it. That wasn't *my* doing."

"But still, you're the one who left her behind." Morgan hummed a few bars of a tune he recognized: George Strait's "This is Where the Cowboy Rides Away."

"Give me a break," he said.

"The pattern continues. I'm afraid nothing's ever going to work out for you."

"Oh, are you?" For some reason he couldn't name, his annoyance was suddenly gone, and he couldn't help grinning. When he saw her face turning pink, he was happy to an unreasonable degree.

"I won't take no for an answer," he told her, when they were sitting down with beers. The bar was constructed to look like a pirate ship had plowed through the wall, and they were sitting on the starboard side, facing the stage. The dance floor teemed with the Columbus Day weekend crowd, including the three pairs of Morgan's guests, who all waved but kept their distance, thank God. Uriah, too, when he poked his head out from the kitchen, just waved. Good. Jesse wanted to be alone with Morgan, not watching her play hostess to everyone.

Then he spotted Jack Harrison coming through the crowd toward them. Of course. It had been too much to hope everyone could just leave them alone for five minutes. "Morgan!" Jack said. "Have you spoken to the DuPages? I was expecting some kind of blowback from the husband, but I haven't heard anything more since Thursday. I just want to make sure things aren't getting out of hand, here, and that they aren't harassing you."

"No, nobody's said anything to me. And I decided I need to focus my attention on the contest." Morgan laughed. "Which, obviously, is why I'm *here* tonight."

Jack laughed, too, and chucked her shoulder. "You deserve to relax a little, Morgan. And you *look* fantastic. I've never seen you all dressed up."

"Oh, stop," Morgan said, blushing. "I'm self-conscious enough as it is."

"I'm just glad Jesse here has convinced you there's more to life than working, even in the busy season." Jack gave Jesse a warm grin.

"I'm trying to get her to sing with me," Jesse said – a subtle way of telling Jack they'd talked enough shop for the night.

"Oh, yes, by all means! I can't wait to hear you again." Jack had gotten Jesse's message, and backed away, his eyes sparking. "You two have a good night."

Jesse was glad he was gone, but he was also glad to think Morgan's neighbors were watching out for her. "Boy, people really do look after each other out here, don't they? That's nice."

"It *is* nice. It's taken you this long to realize it?"

He shrugged. "I've been too damn cold to see straight. Okay, back to business. Now, I *will* give you first song choice. Any duet you want."

Morgan started looking around the room, as if in search of rescue. "I don't see Lainey and Brick, do you? Lainey told me they'd meet us."

When they'd finished on the roof today, Jesse had asked Brick *not* to show up, but he wouldn't be telling Morgan that. Nor would he tell her how Brick had grinned and said, "How's that job I offered you looking now?"

Now Jesse said, "Don't try to skirt the issue. I told you, I won't take no for an answer."

She looked at him. "If I don't want to sing, I won't."

"Right, but you *do* want to sing. Besides, you already agreed, and you owe me."

She rolled her eyes. "I *don't* really want to sing. However, I can see you're like a dog with a bone, and I guess I do owe you. My choice?"

"Your choice."

She nodded, then got up and flounced off to the signup sheet. He watched her, marveling at the swing of her hair and her hips in that skirt – and at the little smile that was on her face as she made her way back.

As she slid onto her stool beside him, he did not move his knee out of the way, and when her bare knee brushed his jeans, electricity shot up his spine. He left his knee where it was – and, without acknowledging the contact, she left hers, too, touching his lightly under the bar. "What song are we doing?" he asked, trying to seem casual, though his heart was knocking in his chest.

"It's a surprise. But we're next, so you won't have long to wait." Still looking around for Lainey and Brick, she took off her jacket to reveal creamy shoulders, a camisole held up by thin straps, and no evidence of a bra. A desire stronger than any he'd felt in years seized him. His body let him know it, and he found looking away impossible. But he had to, had to let himself be brought back to the room and the terrible duet happening on stage, a tourist couple singing "(I've Had) the

Time of My Life," only neither of them could sing and both were terribly drunk and neither of them looked like anybody that you'd want to have the time of your life *with*, and he focused on these sobering thoughts, so that by the time the tourist couple was taking their bows and Morgan grabbed his hand to lead him up on stage, he was in a reasonable condition to follow, and then he had to force himself not to stare at the way her hair swept over those creamy shoulders.

Everybody cheered them – he indulged for a second in the fantasy that some of the crowd might have heard him last night at the Barnacle – and she was gorgeous in the lights. When he saw the name of the song flash on the screen and heard the opening bars, he laughed. "'Mommas, Don't Let Your Babies Grow Up to Be Cowboys'? Are you Waylon or Willie?"

"You're Waylon, I'm Willie," she said, so when the first words lit up, he started to sing about how impossible it was to try to love a cowboy. When she came in on the second set of lines, her voice made his body warm, and her flirty sideways smile sent his heart racing again. He played to her act, and sang the lines with humor, but deep down he found that he didn't want any of what the song said about cowboys to be true about him. Not anymore.

Especially not the part about how they were always bound to ride off alone.

16

"Want to watch Saturday Night Live?" Jesse asked Morgan when they got back to the B&B. After he'd responded to her first song choice with such a great sense of humor and the crowd had given them a huge ovation, she'd ended up agreeing to three more duets. Hearing his voice blending with hers again had made her feel like he understood something elemental about her, something no one else had ever even sensed. Lainey and Brick had never shown up – she supposed in some misguided attempt to give her alone time with Jesse – and all her guests, as far as she could tell, were safely back in their rooms. All night, she'd been processing the fact that Jesse no longer had a girlfriend back home and getting over how self-conscious she'd felt about getting dressed up. Wearing something other than her usual clothes had ended up making her feel a little bold, a little daring, a little not-quite-herself. The appreciative way Jesse'd been looking at her all night hadn't hurt on that score.

All of which made her think she shouldn't sit in the dark with him now. "I've got things to do in the kitchen, and then I have to get up early."

He looked at the clock. "It's ten, so, no more than twenty minutes in the kitchen. Then put on your p-jays and get back out here."

She was ridiculously happy that he was trying to convince her. "Won't take no for an answer, huh?"

"That's right. You owe me," he teased, and she laughed and went out to the kitchen, where she hurried through her preparations for tomorrow's breakfast, being careful of her clothes. When she passed through the living room, he must have been upstairs. In her bedroom, she searched for her prettiest pajamas, and tried not to think too much beyond that, tried not to question the glow – corny as that sounded, it was the right word – that she felt after the night out with him.

When she emerged wearing a tank top and striped pajama bottoms, he was sitting on the couch. He grinned and patted the seat next to him. "You're so darn cute."

"Cute?" she said, sitting next to him cross-legged, just close enough that her knee brushed his leg – like it had been doing all night under the bar at the Cutthroat. She was surprised that she didn't feel nervous, only happy to be near him. "Is that the best you can do?"

"Fish much?" he said, and she laughed, and then he said, "Yeah, all right, you looked stunning tonight. And now you look cute. Ain't too many women can pull both looks off."

"Aw, shucks," she said, actually embarrassed enough that she had to look away. "I felt silly."

"You looked the farthest thing from that." He reached for her left hand. "I noticed you still wear your wedding ring."

Startled, and suddenly feeling way too vulnerable, she pulled her hand back. She twisted the ring around her finger, considering its gold. "Do you think it's silly?"

"I think any man would be lucky to earn such devotion from you."

"I hear a 'but' at the end of that line."

He sat up straighter, turning to face her slightly. "Well, all right. *But* I *do* think you're depriving the men of the world right now by keeping yourself so hidden." His words picked up speed. "I mean, you looked so wonderful tonight, you'd take any mortal man's breath away. And, might I add, you do that on an everyday basis, without even trying."

She laughed a little, not quite believing he meant that she did that to *him* – notwithstanding the other night in the kitchen.

And notwithstanding the song he'd sung last night at the Barnacle which just might have been about her.

His brow was creased with seriousness. "I mean, aren't you lonely, Morgan?"

She couldn't look away from his eyes. "Jesse, I feel like, if I answer that, we'll only go farther down a road that I thought we'd agreed not to go down."

"Now, that makes me mighty curious as to what your answer is. Anyway, we're already going down that road, right? Sitting here in the dark with our legs touching right now? So why don't you just tell me?"

Her face heated up, but she didn't move her leg away. He had this way of convincing her to take risks she never would have taken normally; of making her want to tell him everything. "Well, I didn't *think* I was lonely," she said carefully.

"I think I hear a 'but' at the end of that line."

She smiled. Twisted her ring again. "Well, I thought I was grieving, I guess. Loneliness from grief. That's different from imagining that anyone on earth could make you less lonely. Which I didn't."

He took that in, nodded once. "So, what about now?"

Liking the way he listened to her, the way he really *paid attention,* she took a deep breath and decided to dive in. "Well, since you got here, I realized I'd *been* lonely – and, now that you're here, I'm not." She knew she'd just bounded about a mile down that road she'd just been saying they shouldn't go down – and the amazed look on his face didn't ease her fears. "Not lonely, I mean," she added, out of nerves. "You've made me trust you. And when we sing together… well, there's just never been anything like that, for me."

"Well," he said, and her heart was in her throat. "That is very good news."

"It is?"

"Yes."

"I wasn't sure. Because, I mean, you're leaving. And all of the other things we talked about. Except your girlfriend; I guess that's no longer an issue." She was talking too much, nervous.

"I'm in no big hurry to leave." He was looking at her mouth again.

"Good," she said, and, slowly, she leaned closer to him, tired of holding back. Maybe Lainey and Hannah were right and she just needed to get Jesse out of her system – if that was possible.

He leaned in, too. He smelled of campfire smoke and autumn. His breath was sweet, and their lips touched. Lightly at first, then more insistently. Then he threaded his fingers through her hair and pulled her closer in a way that made her feel weak in the best possible way, and when his tongue touched hers, she was stunned, and, suddenly, she wanted everything.

Kissing him still, she got to her knees and straddled him. He grabbed her hips and pulled her in, and they both gasped when they felt each other through the thin fabric of her pajamas and the rougher grain of his jeans. She pressed against the length of his body, kissing him like nothing else existed in the world. Two seconds more and she was reaching for his belt buckle.

He grabbed her wrists, turned his head away. "Morgan, wait. Wait. What are we doing?"

"What?" She was breathless, like she'd just gone all out on a sprint. She freed her wrists, took his beautiful face in her hands and turned his head back toward her, leaning close again to kiss him. The heat between them, she could feel how much they wanted each other, and she felt like they were strapped inside one of those giant clear Zorb balls tumbling down a hill, helpless but to just enjoy the ride, even as it scared and thrilled and disoriented them.

But he turned his head again, almost imperceptibly, just enough to stop her.

Just enough to make her see that he was under complete control of himself, despite the heat between them, despite that she was handing herself to him like a boiled lobster on a platter.

At that, she wanted to jump up and run into her bedroom and shut the door, pretend this hadn't happened. But he was still holding her hips.

"If you want to stop, Jesse," she said, trying to be calm, "let me go."

His eyes were sincere, deep enough to get lost in all over again. "I couldn't keep from kissing you, but…" He winced, but his hands stayed tightly on her hips, and that together with the softness on his face told her she wasn't being rejected, not exactly, and she wanted to stay and hear what he had to say, though there was still such heat between them that it was difficult to concentrate, and looking at his mouth she just wanted to kiss him again.

She made herself stay back. "What is it, Jesse?"

"Jesus, this is not easy," he said, "and if you'd've told me earlier tonight that we'd be in this position, I would not have thought that I would do this, but… Okay. Here it is: Morgan, the thing is, I can't do this with you unless we're going to do this for real."

Now, on top of everything else, she was confused. "What do you mean? Of course it would be real. How could it not be?" Without quite meaning to, she looked down at where their bodies met, at the wonderful bulge in his jeans.

He laughed a little and put a finger under her chin to lift her gaze. His eyes were intensely blue again. "I don't mean that. I mean… us." Under her, his body rose and fell as he took a deep breath, and he looked up at the ceiling. "I mean, I would, by all that's holy I *would*, want to do this if we were going to try to make something work between us. Like, I mean, I guess I mean: a relationship." He looked at her like he couldn't believe he'd said it.

Neither could she. "What?"

He was clearly warming up to the idea. "That's right. A relationship. I'm *not* just going to sleep with you then ride off," he said, and she could see he was suddenly and absolutely determined.

She leaned back, flabbergasted. Who'd ever heard of a guy saying he wouldn't sleep with you unless you committed to him first? And it was news to her that he even *wanted* a relationship. Was this the same Jesse she knew? "The stories I've heard about Jesse Stewart are not proving to be true."

He laughed, shook his head a little.

"But… how?" she said. "Are you talking about, like, long distance? I mean, I didn't think… You never said…"

"I don't know what I'm talking about, Morgan. Fact is, I'm more attracted to you than I've been to anyone. Like, ever. But what I also know is that you're a girl who's still wearing her wedding ring six years later. Which means, when you give, you give all. So, believe it or not, I really…" He squeezed his eyes shut for a second, then opened them again. "I really care about you, and not just because of Rick. In fact, as far as I'm concerned, he's the elephant in the room right now, but I'm just damned if I'm going to let you give your precious self to me without being a hundred percent certain you'd at least give a shot to letting me give you what you need

153

back. Because I couldn't live with myself if I thought I hurt you."

His sweetness made her want to kiss him again – but what he'd said was too important not to respond to. "But, Jesse, I don't see how we could have a relationship. I live here and you live in North Carolina."

"I know that, Morgan. I just think it might be worth exploring some possibilities…" He seemed, suddenly, to be floundering.

She jumped in to save him. "Jesse, I'm more attracted to you than I have been to anyone, too. I mean, I haven't even been tempted in six years, and ever since you showed up it's been temptation every time I look at you or walk by you or… anything!" She gestured to the position she was in. "You can see what I mean."

He laughed, seeming to appreciate her attempt to leaven the mood.

But she owed him the truth, too, since that was what he was giving her. "So tonight, finally, I don't know… we've been getting along so well. Maybe I was thinking this would make us both feel… like we'd made the most of our time together. Even if that time is shorter than we might like it to be! I mean, if it can't be more, if I can only feel this way for a short time, then maybe… maybe *that's* what I need?" Again, without exactly meaning to, she looked down at that bulge in his jeans, which was no less enchanting than before.

He groaned. "Morgan, you're killing me, here." He lifted her chin again. "Listen, I *know* you – you've *let* me know you, these last couple weeks – and I know that isn't true. You might want this now, but I'm just afraid you'd regret it later. And, like it or not, it could never mean nothing. Because we aren't just any two people, here, right? I'm supposed to be Rick's best friend, and it's been putting me through the wringer, feeling so goddamned attracted to you, and first I wanted to leave because of it, and then I *didn't* want to leave because of it. But still – we can't just thoughtlessly do this."

Everything he said made her feel even warmer toward him that she had. "But I see you're *you*, and I understand that Rick is gone. Maybe more than I ever have, I understand that. I don't think I'd regret –"

He shook his head. "Yes, you would. And I'm here to help you, not hurt you. No matter *how* attracted I am to you, or you to me." He laughed. "Make no mistake, I would love to be with you like that, Morgan. I just don't think having sex with you would be the right thing to do right now." A short laugh again. "Look at that, you're making me into a better man, here."

Instead of being nice to hear, that last line felt like the nail in the coffin. His hold on her hips had lessened, and she quickly twisted off his lap and stood up. "Well, now I'm embarrassed. The man who'll sleep with every girl under the sun won't sleep with me."

His face showed sudden anger. "Now, there. See what I mean? See what you think of me? After everything I just told you? Was that what all this was about? Here I am putting my heart on the line and you're just…. hard up?"

What a disaster. How could she have been so stupid, going straight for the belt buckle like that, then looking down at him twice (even if she hadn't meant to) when he was trying to really *talk* to her – like sex was all she wanted; like he was just some stud here to satisfy a lonely widow? If she had to cross that line, after all this time of holding back, why couldn't she have let everything unfold naturally, shown him she was ready for more, if he was? She'd known how fragile their situation was, yet she'd let her hunger for him get the best of her.

And then to say something so hurtful! But *she* was hurt that he was turning her away, despite all he'd said – and even if maybe he was right, because maybe her heart was too invested with him already, and maybe if they slept together her heart would end up broken when he got on the boat to leave.

As he inevitably would.

Because what kind of relationship could they have, honestly, when they led such different lives? No matter how much she admired him; no matter how good it was to sing with him? She'd kissed him because she was over-the-top attracted to him, yes, but also because she'd been indulging in the kind of wishful thinking she'd promised Lainey she *wasn't* indulging in.

Well, she would just have to stop that – from here on out.

"I don't think those things about you," she said, her stomach aching. "I really don't. And you don't deserve to be spoken to that way. My feelings are just hurt. My pride's injured. I'm sorry. And, yes, I do desire you. A lot. I'm sorry. But look at you!"

He took that in and, after a moment, to her relief, his face softened. "I suppose I can understand that," he said, a spark in his eye again.

She let out a short laugh. "Of course you can. Only you don't feel the same way."

He held out his arm, gesturing for her to sit down next to him again. "Morgan, baby, now that is not true. You can *see* it isn't," he joked, and now *he* glanced down at his lap, "even after all this talking. Don't be hurt, all right? If anything, your pride should be sky-high."

"Why's that?" She stood with her arms folded, fearing that if she took him up on his invitation to sit down again, the same sort of trouble might ensue. Kissing him, being close to him, had been so amazing, and her body was still charged with the feeling.

"Because even though you're the most beautiful woman who's ever come near me, I respect you so much that I didn't take advantage of the opportunity."

Rick might as well have been in the room with them, then. For once, she wished he wasn't. "I suppose you're looking for a medal."

"Would be nice." Jesse reached for the remote and clicked the TV on. "I'd settle for you sitting down here with me and watching Saturday Night Live, as we had previously discussed."

She was amazed – after all that? – and suddenly even more infatuated with him than she'd been. Infatuation – well, that seemed all right, and innocent enough, even with Rick's best friend. At least feeling these things reminded her she was still alive. Making love with Jesse would have been amazing in the short term, but staying friends would be better in the long term. He was the wrong man for her to climb back in the saddle with – she just had to keep reminding herself. "Really?"

"Long as you promise not to climb in my lap again."

She couldn't help but laugh. She sat down beside him, and his arm settled comfortably over her shoulder, and he felt warm and right next to her side as he turned the TV to the right channel, and soon they were laughing together, and soon after that she dozed off, and later the light was out and Jesse was beside her on the narrow couch, pulling the blanket over them, and when she roused herself to protest, he cupped her head in his big hand, kissed her forehead and said, "Hush, Morgan, baby, sleep," and, never having felt so safe in her life, she did, though not before she heard him whisper, "Just think about it… how good it could be."

17

In the morning, to Jesse's dismay, Morgan wasn't with him when he woke up, though the sky was only just beginning to lighten. When he made his way out to the kitchen, she was up to her ears in canisters and jars of things, with a big mixing bowl in front of her, and the fact that she was already dressed in her customary white shirt and green pants made him feel like he'd lost her, when they'd been so close just hours ago. She'd clearly put every one of her walls back up, when last night she'd been ready to tear them all down, and he wondered, if he'd done differently, if there was any chance she'd've let down those walls for good. "Hey," he said, rubbing his forehead to wake himself up. "Early bird."

She dumped a cup of flour into the bowl. "I have to let this bread rise while I'm making breakfast and get it baked this morning. I'll have one more recipe for you to taste around lunchtime."

"Cool." He wanted to talk about last night; wanted to know how she was feeling about everything. About him. "Sleep okay?"

She stirred, not looking up. "Yep!" Not acknowledging that she'd slept beside him; that she'd left him before he was awake.

"Morgan, you're not mad at me, are you?"

She set down her spoon, reached into the bowl with both hands, and plopped a lump of dough onto the floury surface of the counter. "Why would I be mad? You were right." She began kneading.

He walked to her and put a hand on her arm to stop her. She looked at him, and in her eyes he saw sadness, longing.

Unless he was just making that up.

Still, she looked so beautiful, her face smudged with flour, that he wanted to kiss her, say to hell with every last one of the reservations he'd had last night, and take her to bed this morning, in the sober light of day. "Morgan, I – "

Her wry smile curbed his ambitions. "It's all right, Jesse," she said. "There's just too much working against us. We're better off just staying friends. Not talking about … about dreams of anything being different."

"Morgan…"

She shook her head, rested a flour-covered hand on his. "Jesse, you… you mean a lot to me, you know. I would never have imagined when you showed up here how close we'd get in such a short time. That isn't anything I want to jeopardize. And sleeping next to you last night was… well, I haven't felt so taken care of in all my life."

"I wish – "

Another shake of her head, an increased pressure of her hand, stopped him. "You've done me the great favor of showing me that I *can* feel things again," she said. "I can't thank you enough for that."

His heart was in his throat, all his hope and disappointment mixing into a great stew of longing to kiss her again. But that would've probably been counter-productive, since it would make him seem like he hadn't heard a word she'd just said, so he just grinned. "Well, I'm not leaving yet, so don't think you're done being taken care of. Believe I've got a roof to finish, meals to taste, a mole to find and get off the island, a competitor to bust down, and a gig at the Barnacle Wednesday night. Man, I'm busier than a one-legged man in a butt-kicking contest. More than I was back home, that's for sure. How'd you manage to get me so roped in, here, Morgan?"

She smiled and went back to kneading her bread. "Maybe you like it."

"It's *cold* here," he said.

She laughed.

Sunday and Monday passed in a blur. Jesse and Brick worked on the roof, with Paul and Jack Harrison helping as much as they could. Morgan cooked and cleaned non-stop, making everything perfect for Ally's arrival. Jesse tasted her final recipe – French toast made of challah bread, drenched in homemade egg nog with a touch of rum, then baked with blueberries and served with maple syrup – and declared it spectacular. They ate dinner together Sunday night and laughed and laughed over some of his stupid stories. He hoped she'd stay on the couch with him again that night, but, with a look of what he thought might be regret, she claimed exhaustion and disappeared into her room.

On Monday, the Columbus Day weekend guests all left on the afternoon boat, leaving the B&B – and the whole island – feeling deserted. Jesse and Brick worked till after dark finishing up the final details on the roof, and Jesse was relieved they'd managed to accomplish what Morgan needed. With a wink and a smile, Brick begged off Jesse's invitation to come inside, and Jesse went in to find Morgan had made dinner again. Alone in the house for the first time ever, they toasted their success at making the B&B "photo-ready" in time, and laughed a great deal more while they ate. He cleaned up the kitchen while she made fresh bread dough that she'd let rise overnight.

She'd said he could stay in one of the guest rooms upstairs, now that they were empty, but he'd declined. "I'm kinda settled in, seems silly to move right now," he'd told her, though the truth was he just didn't want to put himself farther away from where she was. But after going up to shower and brush his teeth, he found himself alone in the living room, disappointed because it seemed she'd gone to bed without saying good night.

Well, so it went, and he was going to have to get used to the fact that he couldn't stay here forever. With the roof done, after his gig on Wednesday night, he'd have no excuse to stay, and he knew his dad needed him at work. Buster needed him, too. Besides, it was clear Morgan was pretty determined they were never going to be anything more than friends.

But he was going to miss this place, that was for sure – more than he'd ever thought possible. The other night when Jack Harrison had come up to Morgan at the Cutthroat to check in about Woods and Water, Jesse had realized he'd never experienced such a strong sense of community. That and the way people had pitched in to get the word out about Woods and Water and help him finish the roof made think a person could do worse than to try to make a life here.

Even if it was ridiculously cold.

He sighed and pulled out his guitar and notebook. He was scratching some lines about futility, then scratching them out, when Morgan came out of her room in her pajamas and sat down on the couch next to him, like that was the most natural thing in the world to do.

Thrilled, he tried not to react, just reached over his guitar to set his notebook on the coffee table in front of him, taking in the pretty sight of her. "So, ten thirty tomorrow morning," she said, like they'd been in the middle of a conversation, "Ally gets here. Why do I feel so calm?"

He shrugged, smiled a little. It was all he could do not to lean over and kiss her, consequences be damned. He strummed his guitar instead. "Maybe because you know you're ready."

She laughed. "It's ridiculous, really. I'm going to serve her things I've made only once before and served only to you. You'd tell me if they weren't good, right?"

"Of course I would."

She looked at him, and his desire for her intensified.

He needed to distract himself. *Just friends, remember?* he told himself, though, being back on this couch with her, all he could seem to think of was her straddling his lap the other night. He had to stop that. He strummed his guitar again. "Nobody in the house but us, right?" he said. "So I can play?"

She nodded, and her eyes were bright.

"Hey, you know this one?" he said, playing the opening strains of Vince Gill's song "Go Rest High on that Mountain."

"Yes," she said, looking startled.

"Sing it with me," Jesse said, and started in on the verse. Then he felt pretty stupid, because it was a mourning song. He hadn't even thought of that. He'd just been thinking about the cool harmonies.

But she was smiling a little as he sang, so he kept on, and when she came in on the harmonies, the beauty of the sound wasn't just doubled; it plain skyrocketed. She gave him chills, made him feel things he didn't know were in him to feel.

Yet he knew the song couldn't help but make her think of Rick. Jesse was thinking of Rick, too.

But they kept on singing, smiling encouragement to each other, both their voices breaking at times. His vision blurred with unexpected tears, and, by the time they sang the last notes, her face was coated in hers.

She wiped them away. "Sorry," she said, though she didn't look embarrassed so much as totally vulnerable.

Jesse shook his head, telling her it was all right. "You know, he wouldn't want you to be so sad, after all this time."

"You're sad, too!"

He shrugged, played the opening chords of Garth Brooks's "Two of a Kind, Workin' on a Full House." She laughed a little, wiping her face again.

"Hell," he said then, inspired, "you should come to Nashville *with* me." He couldn't help it. It was a pipe dream, anyway, so why not go all out with it? "Your voice is so pretty."

"What?"

"You used to dream of making it, too, right?"

"A long time ago."

He shrugged again, started the intro to a new song, an up-tempo version of "Will the Circle be Unbroken."

"Still," he said. "Let's not be sad. Deal?" She nodded once, looking determined. He started singing the first verse, and was glad to see her smile.

She joined him every time on the chorus, and, by the time they'd finished, they both were laughing – and he was feeling even more desire for her than he had.

So distracting himself with music wasn't going to work. He finished with a flourish then set his guitar aside, and saw she looked a little disappointed.

That seemed good to him, because he, too, felt he could go on singing with her forever.

"So, what's next for you?" he said. "After this contest?"

"Ha," she said, wiping her eyes again. With the thought of her present life, she seemed to switch right back to her old self. "Something I've hardly thought about. Well, I'm open weekends and holidays through New Year's."

He was regretting bringing it up. "Sounds kinda backward to me. What do you do the rest of the time?"

165

"Finish cleaning up the garden and getting it ready for next year. Plant a hundred tulip bulbs in the front. Then marketing, deep cleaning. Usually some redecorating projects. I'm a big fan of redecorating. I'm closed January through April, so, this year, maybe I'll be adding the bathrooms, if this contest turns out in my favor. And I'll have to figure out what to do about Woods and Water."

He let that all sink in, and it didn't sound that good to him. "You know, Fayetteville's nice that time of year. I've been thinking of buying a nice little house. Maybe a little farm, or at least a place with room for a big garden. I got a little money saved up. Just hadn't gotten around to it yet. Speaking of pipe dreams."

Twisting up her hair, she laughed, as if the only way she could take that was as a joke. "I thought we weren't going to talk about things like that. Dreams."

He shrugged, not wanting to push too hard and make her shut down again, because he liked the way she was smiling at him now. "You know me and rules. Besides, you're the one who came out to sit by me."

Her smile deepened. "I just wanted to see what was on TV."

With a groan of pretend exasperation, he wrapped his arm around her shoulders, pulled her close and turned on the TV. Noise filled the room, breaking some of the tension that had been welling up inside him. Probably a good thing. "Happy?" he said.

"Very." She leaned on his shoulder. "You don't mind, do you? If you do, just say so and I'll go back in my room."

"I don't mind a bit," he said, and later, with her asleep on his shoulder, he turned out the light and the TV and got her to stretch out beside him.

But as he pulled the blanket over them, she roused, trying to sit up. "I should go to my room. I'm sorry for coming out here. I just wanted to be in the same room you were. And I'm glad we sang."

The sweetness of that knifed his heart. Gently, he pulled her down beside him. "I want to be in the same room you are," he said.

"Are you sure? It isn't too confusing?"

"I don't care." He wrapped his hand around her waist, only too late realizing her tank top had inched up and his hand was on her warm bare skin. He tried to move it, to pull her shirt down, but her hand pressed his back onto her skin.

"I just keep getting more attached to you," she whispered.

"I don't mind a bit."

"Did you really mean it about Fayetteville? I could come? Or –" She smiled. "Nashville?"

His heart ker-thunked. "Yeah." He wanted to ask her if she would, or which one she'd be more likely to actually do, but he still didn't want to push her.

She touched his face. She kissed him. Softly at first, like a thank you. But the second kiss was more like a question. As he answered, kissing her back, he could feel himself surrendering, and when their tongues touched, it was like being struck by lightning. "Jesse," she whispered. "Just for tonight, let's not be who we are."

He kissed her again, harder, half angry that *that* would be the way she'd ask him, and half carried away by desire and not caring what words she chose. And then he didn't think anymore, and, some moments later, he was the one to unbutton his jeans and guide her hand to him, and she drew in a breath and said, "Oh, my." Then she had her pajamas off and he was reaching for his wallet on the end table and the condom inside, and then he was kneeling over her, touching her and saying, "Are you sure?"

"Yes, please," she said, and he found her, gently at first, slowly, and then deeply, and she pulled him to her and they moved together till the stars shattered and fell, and then they laughed and laughed, in happiness and surprise.

"Something came over me," she said, running a finger down his tattooed arm while his breath ruffled her hair. She'd never felt so satiated and so revved up at once. Thoughts and doubts of both the present and the past had been blotted out by pleasure. "I think it was you."

"*I* think you been storing that up a while." She could hear the smile in his drowsy voice.

"You aren't going to sleep, are you?" She thought she'd be lonely, if he did. Singing with him had broken her open, and making love had done something even more profound than that.

He moved his warm hand across her body, sending her already pleased nerve endings into overdrive. "Hold your horses one second and I'll be right back with you."

She laughed and kissed him, wanting nothing more than for this night to just go on and on.

18

"Here she is!" Jesse announced late the next morning, walking in the door with two big Coach suitcases. Behind him came a gorgeous, tall blond woman, probably twenty-eight years old, gleaming hair down to her waist, expensive sunglasses propped on her head, big blue eyes with spiky lashes, and a muscular, trim body that suggested she did Pilates every waking moment. Morgan's heart sank. This was Ally? For God's sake.

"You certainly have the best welcoming committee so far," Ally said, holding out a gloved hand for Morgan to shake, even as she batted her eyes at Jesse. "And I don't have to keep that a secret."

"Well, good." Morgan smiled, keeping her jealousy hidden. She and Jesse hadn't woken up till after eight, which had left no time at all for talking, since she had to make the bread and he had to finish putting away the scaffolding and cleaning up the remnants of the roof project – except he'd kissed her hand and said, "You can move to Fayetteville, baby, but you're going to have to take off this wedding ring. My reputation couldn't take the scandal, otherwise."

That, of course, had totally freaked her out – had she agreed to move to Fayetteville? Did he mean full-time? Give up her business and everything she'd worked so hard for? And the thought of taking off Rick's ring – well, this was the first time she'd even had cause to consider it, so it was no wonder the idea made her nervous.

But to have a woman like Ally in front of Jesse's nose right now seemed like the worst possible timing. These next couple of days, just the three of them would be in the house, and Morgan was already feeling crowded, insecure, and unsure – what with the way Jesse was smiling at Ally right now – whether he'd actually *liked* being with Morgan last night, or if she'd just happened to be the only woman available on the island.

Or at least the only one taking off her clothes and saying, "Yes, please."

And maybe the worst part was, now she *knew* what all the fuss was about, why women kept flocking to him and putting up with his bad behavior. The man not only had excellent attributes, he also knew things.

Things which, even now, made her flush to think of.

And she'd thought she had a bad case for Jesse *before...*

Not that she could say any of this, of course. "Let's get you settled in, Ally, and I'll have the first breakfast ready in half an hour, if that suits you."

"You bet," Ally said. "I know it's a little odd, serving breakfast at eleven, but with the boat schedule and *my* schedule, that was the only way it could work. One breakfast today and one each of the next two mornings,

then you'll get me off the island on Thursday, right?"
Great, and she was *nice*, too.

"That's right, we've made arrangements for one of
our lobstermen to take you to the mainland, since you
said you had to get going early. The ferries don't leave
until afternoon."

"Oh, thank you, that's just great. I can't wait to eat!
Rob, my editor, just raved about this place, and it is so
beautiful."

Jesse broke in with one of his knee-weakening
smiles. "Let me show you to your room, Ally, and get
these things up there for you."

She turned to him with a megawatt smile of her own.
"I would *love* that, Jesse. Thanks."

"See you back down here in a few minutes!"
Morgan called after them, as Ally followed Jesse to
the stairs.

Watching them disappear together, overhearing Ally
laugh uproariously at something Jesse had said, Morgan
was overcome with jealousy again.

But making Ally's visit great was the goal, of course,
and Jesse was only doing exactly what Morgan had asked
him to, charming the woman so she'd have a good experience. If Ally ended up charming *him* in return, that
would probably be no more than Morgan deserved for
not listening to all those reasons why not that she'd told
herself about a million times.

Anyway, she had no time to wallow in misery. She had
French toast to bake, a plate to prepare, and the taste and
presentation had to be the best she'd ever created.

"So he isn't your husband? Your partner?" Ally said earnestly, having polished off a big plate of baked blueberry French toast while she made notes in indecipherable handwriting.

"No," Morgan said, hating the implication of Ally asking that, even as she poured her another cup of coffee. "He's just been here helping me for a couple weeks. Autumn chores, you know." A mental flash of last night made her ears hot.

"Boy, good friend," Ally said. She smiled and sipped her coffee, the look on her face transparently hopeful.

As Morgan cleared Ally's empty plate, she was thinking of how it had been to sing with him last night, just the two of them, their voices blending through her whole body, her whole *self.* "Yes, he sure is. He was my husband's best friend. He and I are pretty close, actually."

This passed right over Ally's head. "And he's single?"

Morgan wanted to kick something. "Well, he's kinda, um, what do people say? He's 'talking to' someone, I think."

"Oh." Ally looked distressed. "But it isn't anything serious?"

Morgan felt slightly sorry for the girl, then; she'd clearly been bitten by the Jesse bug.

And it wasn't like Morgan had the right to keep Jesse from exercising his free will, no matter what had happened last night. She'd been the one, after all, to suggest that they pretend they weren't themselves, so who knew whether he thought what they'd done in the night had any impact whatsoever on what happened today. That thing about her moving to Fayetteville had maybe just been one of his smartass jokes. "I don't know," she said, and, in an effort to change the subject, added, "You're not married?"

"No." Ally sighed. "Living in New York City, you know. Not exactly marriage central."

Morgan smiled, relieved. "Well, Jesse's a country boy from North Carolina. He's got such deep roots there you can practically see them growing out of his boots. I doubt you'd have much in common with him, being a city girl."

"Oh, I don't know. I grew up in a small town. I miss it sometimes. I don't guess I'll live in New York forever. I mean, who knows what fate has in store for us, right? Or when we'll cross paths with the right person?" She was looking hopeful again.

Damn it. And why did she have to be so *sweet?*

Just then, Jesse came in from the back of the house, bringing with him the crisp smell of the outdoors. He'd been, as he put it, "prettying up" the garden a bit more while Ally ate. Now he treated Ally to one of his grins. "How was the French toast? Best you ever had in your life, right?"

Ally grinned back. "That's confidential. So how about showing me around the island, like you promised?"

"Sure thing. First, Morgan, I wanted to tell you, word on the dock was old Caleb Brown got his foot stuck in a line out on his boat this morning and broke his leg. He was by himself since his sternman was sick, but he was able to get to his radio, and Tim Sawyer got him to the mainland."

"Oh, God, is he going to be okay?"

"Word was he was still on his way to the hospital, cussing up a storm."

"Well, that puts things in perspective, I guess."

"Sure does." His eyes looked deep.

Ally had picked up her camera and slung the strap around her neck. She tossed her hair. "You ready, Jesse?"

Before Morgan knew it, they were gone, and the wink Jesse gave her on the way out the door didn't make her feel any better.

That night, Ally insisted on a bonfire and a private concert by Jesse, after he'd told her about the bonfires they'd been having. Morgan, still trying to make sure Ally had a good time, ran to Island General for S'mores supplies and called all her friends. By seven o'clock, everyone was gathered around and Jesse was singing, while Morgan endured the sight of Ally in a fluffy white coat sitting next to him on the log in the flickering light of the flames, gazing adoringly at him and taking every chance to touch his arm – or leg – between songs, as she made her requests or praised or teased him.

Morgan guessed she had only herself to blame, since Jesse had asked her half a dozen times to sing with him and she'd refused. The whole crowd had urged her on, but she'd stood firm, not sure she'd be able to handle her emotions, especially after last night. But now, watching Ally, Morgan half wished she'd taken the chance and said yes.

"She looks like a snowflake," Hannah whispered, disgust in her voice, as Jesse launched into another song. She and Morgan and Lainey were standing on the opposite side of the fire from where Jesse and Ally sat, so there was little chance Ally could have heard her, but still, Morgan didn't want to say too much. She hadn't told her friends about last night, and she wasn't going to.

"I know. At least it seems like she's having a good time."

Lainey shook her head. "Oh, Morgan."

"Well, what am I supposed to do? He's leaving the island after his gig at the Barnacle tomorrow. If he wants to spend time with Ally, who claims to be a small town girl who'd leave New York City for the right man, who am I to stop him?"

Lainey sipped her tea. "Um, the woman he's in love with?"

"Yeah, really," Hannah said.

Jesse was singing about somebody's pretty smile while looking right at Ally, smiling that smile of his own that had so recently turned Morgan inside out. She could see it was having a similar effect on Ally.

"Does he honestly look like he's in love with me?" she whispered, her stomach aching as flashes of last night plagued her mind. "*I* think he looks like he's about to prove everything I thought about him being a cowboy true."

"Want me to beat her up?" Hannah joked, but Lainey said nothing, and when Morgan looked at her, she had a look on her face that was half puzzlement, half a frown.

"Hey, did you guys hear any news about Caleb?" Morgan asked, just to take her mind off her own misery.

"Oh!" Lainey was jolted out of whatever she was thinking about Jesse. "It was a clean break, thank goodness. But he'll be laid up a while. His grandson's coming out to stay with him and take over his traps for the rest of the season. I guess he doesn't live too far away, so he'll be here tomorrow."

"Well, that's good news."

"Oo," Hannah said. "Another man who smells like bait to populate the island."

Lainey laughed. "I think he's single. Sure you don't want to stay? Forsake that city guy of yours?"

"Tempting." Hannah tossed her gleaming dark hair. "But not likely. Not too many more days and I'm apt to be engaged, ladies."

That comment brought Morgan, somehow, back to the center of her misery. Here Lainey might be pregnant, Hannah was getting engaged – and Morgan was just standing here watching this perfect girl, Ally, move in on the man who, even if he wasn't in love with her, Morgan was pretty sure she was falling in love with.

Morgan wasn't surprised when, as things were drawing to a close and Jesse announced this would be his last song, she saw Ally lean close to his ear and whisper something that made him smile. But she *was* surprised when he said something back that made Ally frown. He began to sing, and he wasn't done with the first verse when Ally stood and made her way to Morgan. "Guess I'll turn in for now," she said. "Thanks for everything. The S'mores were delicious."

"Oh! Do you need a flashlight to get back to the house?"

"No, it's fine, thanks. See you in the morning!"

As she left, Hannah leaned in to Morgan and whispered gleefully, "Shot down cold."

It certainly looked that way, but Morgan wasn't sure. She kept an eye on Jesse as they bid everyone good night and put out the fire and carried everything inside to the kitchen. She'd already prepared everything that she could ahead of time for the apple-rosemary crepes she'd be making in the morning – cooking for one person instead of six actually felt ridiculously easy, even if the stakes were high – so she followed Jesse into the living room.

"So what did you say to Ally that made her so unhappy?" she asked him, keeping her voice low.

He flopped onto the couch, maddeningly hard to read. "Just that I had to get some shuteye, keep my voice in good form for tomorrow night. She wanted to take a walk."

"Oh."

"That all right? I know you wanted me to show her a good time." The smirk on his face showed that he knew Morgan had never expected Ally to be so beautiful.

"Yes, of course. Of course it's all right." She felt suddenly nervous. "I just didn't know… well, I wouldn't want what we've…" *Had? Been?* No, neither was right. "I wouldn't want to keep you from anything you might want to do."

He grinned and laced his hands behind his head. "I'll keep that in mind."

This was not, she realized, what she'd wanted him to say, and she knew suddenly that she was in way deeper with him than she wanted to be. Ha, so much for pretending she wasn't herself last night. She had been with him fully, truly. It really was going to kill her when he left, wasn't it? Regardless of what might or might not happen between him and Ally.

Maybe, in fact, it would be good if something did happen – maybe that would bring Morgan crashing back to what she knew was reality: Jesse wasn't the type to stick around or commit to any one woman, and his comments about Morgan moving to Fayetteville or Nashville with him had surely just been jokes.

And if she *was* falling in love with him, she'd better catch herself, and quick.

"She seems sweet," she said.

"I guess so," he said, and his smile faded. He lowered his hands and leaned forward. "Morgan, you know, singing one song with me wouldn't have killed you tonight."

She wasn't so sure.

When she said nothing, he sighed. "I hope you know, I'm not – "

"Well, good night, Jesse," she interrupted. She just couldn't stand to hear what he had to say. *I'm not serious about you moving to Fayetteville?* Or, possibly worse, *I'm not playing around about you moving to be with me?*

Because what on earth would she do then, if he *wasn't* joking? She couldn't really spend winters in Fayetteville. That was just impossible. She had too much work to do here. Besides, she couldn't believe that, even if he was serious right now, that the seriousness could last. "Thanks for everything today." She turned to go into her room.

His voice stopped her. "Morgan, you can't just leave. We haven't even talked about last night."

She turned, and he was on his feet, looking angry, and she felt suddenly certain that she'd made a mistake.

Or probably a *few* mistakes – beginning with letting him come here at all. "Jesse, I just... I don't think I'm ready for all of this. You're leaving, and you... well, you seem to like Ally, and, besides, we said we weren't even ourselves – "

He groaned. "Morgan, you could drive a man to his death. It was you I was with. You. And I – "

"Don't say anymore, Jesse, please. You're going to break my heart."

"Why? Why does every scenario in your mind have to end with your heart getting broken? And, can I remind you? You're the one who started it last night."

"That was before Ally got here and you started flirting with her."

"So what? It doesn't mean anything. You told me to show her a good time."

It doesn't mean anything. So how was Morgan supposed to trust that he was being sincere with her? She made herself taller. "I think we should just be friends, Jesse. Like we said before. Anything else is too hard."

"For God's sake, Morgan, life is hard. You're telling me you don't feel – "

"Stop, Jesse, just stop," she said, and she rushed into her room and shut the door, swallowing back tears. She tried to tell herself: He *wasn't* as good a man as she'd believed the past few days, and what they'd had last night could only be a one-time thing. And that was that!

Shaking, leaving the lights off so she wouldn't have to look at her face in the mirror, she got ready for bed and climbed between cold sheets alone.

19

The next night at the Barnacle, Jesse's hands were cold as he climbed onto the stage, and he was tired. He'd stayed up way too late last night writing words to a new song, and he'd spent the morning out at his rock setting it to music, while Morgan fed Ally breakfast and let her take all the pictures of the B&B that she wanted. In the afternoon, Jesse'd ended up taking a long hike around the island with Ally, because Morgan had asked him to, which had totally pissed him off. After everything they'd shared, singing together, making love – Jesse had felt things the other night that he'd *never* felt with anyone else – why was she pretending it had been nothing? Worse, why was she trying to push him off onto someone else?

His plan yesterday – make Ally feel welcome, as Morgan had asked him to, and, in the process, he hoped, make Morgan just jealous enough to make her think that solidifying what they'd started would be a good idea – had backfired spectacularly. Last night, when she'd gone into her room and closed the door, he was just angry and heartbroken and confused enough not to try to follow her. Wanting her with him, he'd written a song instead, and, even after that, he hadn't slept worth a damn.

And Ally was a sweet girl, not to mention beautiful as all get-out, so when she'd asked him to buy her a lobster roll and eat an early supper with her down on the dock tonight as the sun was setting, he'd done it. And they'd had a pretty good time, except for the fact that, on top of being freezing cold, Jesse felt his heart, soul, and body reaching back to where Morgan was, at the warm B&B.

Then it was time for his gig, so he and Ally walked back to get his guitar, Ally snapping more pictures along the way, and Morgan, who'd dressed up for the evening in a black sweater dress that skimmed her curves enough to make any man feel like a race car driver destined for a crash, acted like she was happy they'd stayed gone so long and had a good time. Jesse thought he saw anger in her eyes, but he felt like a fool, anyway, because all he really wanted was to have spent the day with her instead.

Now both women were sitting at a front table, cheering for him, and he didn't know if he should sing the song he'd written last night or not.

He hid his nervousness with a grin as he greeted the crowd and began to sing one of his old songs, a song he knew so well he could perform it almost on auto-pilot, which was a good thing, because every time he looked at Morgan, the stew of anger and betrayal in her eyes nearly made his voice crack, while, next to her, Ally was gazing at him with the hopefulness of a puppy, and Jesse tried not to think he'd been leading her on today.

Then again, he mused as he sang his second song, decidedly *not* looking at either woman for a while, if Morgan was going to insist on pushing him away, it wasn't as if he hadn't had a fine time with Ally today. Maybe he should do what Morgan wanted and move on.

But when after several more songs he took a break and went and sat down with the two of them – at that, he guessed he was like a man who had to stick his head out the door to check if the rain was wet – Ally's fawning annoyed him, and Morgan was so cool and distant – not cold, just smiling at him like they'd never had those nights together, or the long talks, or the moments bonding in the kitchen; like they didn't know each other *at all* – that he couldn't stand it. If he didn't at least try, he'd be doing the exact thing that the song he'd written bemoaned having done last night: letting her walk away.

When he went back on stage, the crowd welcomed him with cheers. "Thanks," he said, pulling a cheat sheet from his pocket and laying it on the floor next to his boot. He had to go for it before he lost his nerve. "Now, here's a little song I wrote pretty recently. I hope you like it." With a glance at Morgan, he began playing the chords he'd worked out this morning and, when the moment came, he started to sing: "I'm kickin' myself right now, watchin' you walkin' out, watchin' you take with you what I need. I could be holdin' you right now, but ever'thing headed south, as I sat and watched your shadow cross the room." Two chords – he couldn't meet her eyes – and then he wailed away on the chorus: "Shadows on my heart, watchin' for the stars, hopin' you'll come back next to me. Shadows on my heart, searchin' where you are, prayin' soon that you'll come back to me."

He chanced a look up and caught a glimpse of Ally looking starstruck and thrilled – did she think it was about her, last night? *Shit* – while Morgan looked something more like bewildered. Well, he was in it now, and had to finish. He kept singing: "You say you want to be friends. Oh, tell me how this ends, when I know for a fact you have what I need. I'm not gonna ride away, no matter what you say. Give me a chance to prove my love's true." Now Ally was beaming and Morgan was wiping at her eye. What a mess. "Shadows on my heart," he sang, really going for it, because it was too late to do anything else. "Waitin' on the stars, waitin' on the time you're next to me. Shadows on my heart, findin' where you are, waitin' for the time you're here with me." He played two chords. "You're here with me." A last one. "Here with me."

The crowd went wild, and Ally was the first to leap to her feet. Everyone else stood up, too, but he would have sworn Morgan was among the last, and she wasn't smiling, as he tipped his hat to the crowd and hoped he hadn't just made the biggest mistake of his life.

After he was all through, a stack of people came up to talk to him, and, when they'd all dispersed, Ally was standing there by herself, grinning to beat the band. "Morgan went ahead," she told him. "Said she had some things to do to get ready for tomorrow's breakfast."

That damn breakfast. He'd be glad if there was never another guest at the inn again, because he was so tired of her always, always having something to do, some excuse to walk away. "All right," he said to Ally, his stomach hurting that Morgan would just up and leave like that when he'd put his heart on the line for her – and she'd have to be completely goddamned clueless not to know.

As they set out walking, Ally linked her arm with his, surprising him. "Oh, Jesse, that new song of yours was so *sweet,* and I saw you look at me before you started it, and Morgan said you'd never played it before.... I mean, I know the second part was kind of fictionalized, but is it too much to hope I might have inspired the first part when I walked out of the bonfire last night?"

He didn't know what to say. *Um, yeah?* But if he hurt Ally's feelings, she might take it out on Morgan in the contest, which was the last thing Jesse wanted, even if he was pissed at her right now. "An artist has to retain some mystery around his work."

Ally squealed. "Oh, I knew it! I knew there was real chemistry here. Jesse." She stopped in her tracks, which made him stop, and she turned to face him and rested her hands on his arms. "I'm going to die if you don't kiss me right now."

"Oh, Jesus," he blurted.

She smiled. "He doesn't need to be involved." She stroked his arms. "Listen, I know you're an old-fashioned guy, and *I'm* an old-fashioned girl, but the fact is that I have to leave tomorrow, and I just don't want to miss out on seeing what we might have."

For a flash, he thought about how easy it would be to fall into something far less complicated than what he had going on with Morgan. About going back to his old way of jumping into bed with a pretty girl the first time she blinked her eyes and smiled – and if that girl lived far away, like Ally did, so much the better, because he could get shed of her afterward fairly easily and without seeming like a complete jerk.

But he thought about what he really wanted. About his dad advising him on the long game. After the night they'd had together, Morgan was obviously a little freaked out. Who wouldn't be, in her shoes? Maybe he just had to try harder to convince her that they could overcome all the things that, as she put it, were stacked against them. He had to talk to her about what their options really were, because time was running out.

First things first, though, he had to get Ally off his back without hurting her feelings or souring her visit to the island.

"Listen," he said gently, "I'm not sure how much you had to drink tonight, but I'm not in the habit of taking advantage of anyone who's beyond their limits even a little bit."

She pouted. "I only had two glasses of wine. I'm not beyond my limits."

He shook his head sadly, like he was some kind of teetotaler who thought any alcohol at all could only have a bad effect on someone's choices. "I know it's your last night, but rushing things never did anybody any good. Let me think of you as the pretty, sweet girl you are, not as someone who I survived some kind of car crash with, all right?" He guessed he had crashing on his mind.

"Oh, Jesse. You're so *sweet*. I can hardly stand it."

He grinned. "Well, you're just going to have to let me walk you back to Morgan's, and that's all there is to it." He started walking again, tucking her hand in his elbow again so she'd follow along.

"Can you eat breakfast with me in the morning?" she said.

"Thought you couldn't be distracted while you're doing your judging duties."

She sighed. "That's right. Well, maybe you could walk me to the boat when I have to leave?"

"I'd be happy to," he said, and they were at the front door of the B&B. "Good night."

She stood on her tiptoes, leaning in. "Aren't you coming in?"

He sneaked out of her range. "Morgan likes for me to use the back door. See you in the morning, all right? Sleep tight."

In the shower in her private bathroom, Morgan was angrily shampooing her hair, and who she was mad at was herself. Of all the stupid, cowardly moves. How could she have *left* the Barnacle, after Jesse had sung that song that was clearly meant for her? But she had. More than that, she'd actually let Ally assume *she'd* been the inspiration for it, and, much like last night at the campfire (only worse!), left the other woman there to swoop in on him, just because she'd asked: "Would you mind if I walked home with Jesse by myself?"

And, Morgan, stupidly, because she was still in "make Ally happy because she's the judge" mode, had just agreed!

Ruing what seemed yet another terrible mistake, she'd waited around in the shadows outside long enough to see them walk out together, see Ally thread her arm through Jesse's like they were an actual couple. *I guess that's that!* Morgan had told herself, and she'd rushed home so they wouldn't see her, ripped off her stupid sweater dress and jumped into the shower to try to wash the whole stupid night off herself.

Because when he'd sung that song, that was way more than she'd bargained for. She had it stuck in her head even now: *I'm not gonna ride away, no matter what you say… Give me a chance to prove my love's true.*

Too good to be true, right? His *love?*

The thought that it *might* be true – not to mention how much she wished it *could* be – had scared her to death.

And now Jesse would no doubt think she was the worst kind of cold-hearted there was, because she'd walked out without responding.

And probably, as a result, he'd be vulnerable to Ally's charms. In fact, the two of them were likely upstairs right now, popping the cork on the bottle of champagne Ally'd bought at Island General this morning and asked Morgan to put in the refrigerator to chill. And what had Morgan said, even though she'd suspected Ally's plans? "Sure, of course! It'll be right here. Just grab it out whenever you want it."

She could've kicked herself now. She was so tired of always putting *other* people's needs and wants above her own.

She couldn't let this happen, could she? Let Jesse and Ally get together, when so much was unresolved between her and Jesse?

So what could she do, now that she'd made a series of disastrous mistakes that had gotten them *here*?

The fire alarm! she thought. She'd light a match near the smoke detector. All the detectors were wired together, so alarms would go off through the whole house. That would definitely get Jesse and Ally out of Ally's room, and then once things calmed down – the mood would be totally spoiled, of course – she could tell Jesse she needed to talk to him. Privately.

Then she could tell him how the song had touched her. How she was willing to give a relationship a try. How she *wanted* to. How she'd certainly *visit* him in Fayetteville this winter, as much and as often as she could. And then they could figure out, in the spring, if they were still happy, what came next.

She couldn't wait to tell him. She just needed to finish rinsing her hair.

In the mudroom, Jesse set down his guitar and kicked off his boots. He didn't know where Morgan was, but he wasn't going to let her push him off any longer. He was going to find her and tell her that he knew she was worth fighting for.

The living room was empty and her bedroom door was ajar. He went over and tapped on it. "Morgan?"

He heard the shower running. Impatient, he decided to knock on the bathroom door and tell her to hurry up and get out. He didn't think they were quite at the point where he could just barge into the bathroom, though the thought of seeing her in the shower was a pleasant one. But they really needed to talk, first.

He'd never been in her bedroom, and he took it in in a glance. Most everything was white, with accents – including about seventeen pillows on the bed – in shades of green. As he neared the bathroom door and turned to knock, something caught his eye. A dresser, against the wall facing the foot of her bed, its top covered with framed photographs of Rick, and of Rick and Morgan.

Jesse moved closer, looking at the familiar face of his best friend. On the wall above the dresser was a page of a letter matted and framed alongside a wedding photo of Rick in his dress uniform and Morgan in her slim strapless dress, the two of them beaming like they'd found the secret to life. Jesse, who'd been the best man at the occasion, recognized Rick's handwriting in the letter: *If anything ever happens to me, know that I'll always be with you, watching over you and loving you.*

The whole artful display was free of dust, and, on the dresser, stuck in among the photographs were two bundles of letters, one tied with a yellow ribbon, one tied with white. Jesse picked them up. Rick's letters to Morgan, and her letters to him. And inside a white-painted wooden box was, from what Jesse could make out, every greeting card the man had ever sent her. *I will love you forever,* he'd written, in most all of them.

Jesse looked at Rick's face again. No wonder Morgan had been hesitant to get involved with anybody, let alone with Jesse. There wasn't a single bone in her body that was ready to move on. Not when she still had this display up – six years later! – where she could see it every morning when she woke up and every night when she went to bed. Here Jesse'd flattered himself that he was breaking her out of her rut; that she actually felt something for him. When, fact was, she was still entirely taken up by the past, by Rick.

So what last night had been, it was suddenly and painfully clear, was strictly physical. Her body wanting Jesse's. Not *her* wanting *him*. "Just for tonight, let's not be who we are," she'd said, and Jesse guessed now that that was the only way she'd been able to go through with it. Pretending to be just a *body*, *any* body, and letting that body do what it wanted with his. Like he'd accused her of that first time she'd tackled him, she'd just been hard up. No wonder she hadn't wanted to talk about it; no wonder she'd looked horrified when he'd mentioned she'd need to take off her ring if she moved to Fayetteville.

Could you actually feel your heart breaking inside your chest? Jesse imagined he could feel his, as he adjusted the things on the dresser to make sure they were exactly as they'd been. *Sorry, buddy, didn't mean to horn in,* he said to Rick, feeling like the world's biggest idiot. He heard the shower turn off. He left the bedroom, shutting the door quietly behind him.

Morgan had hardly been out of the shower two minutes when, her wet hair soaking her bathrobe, she hurried out into the living room – speed was important, what with Jesse probably in Ally's room – ready to grab a match and implement her smoke alarm plan.

Instead, she was astonished to see Jesse, sitting in the rocking chair with a pile of clothes and his open duffel on the floor in front of him. "Jesse?"

"Hey, Morgan." He looked very tired. "Listen, I figured I might as well go with Ally on that lobster boat back to the mainland tomorrow morning."

Morgan's stomach clenched. She suddenly felt very cold. "You're going back with her?" This was far worse than anything she could've imagined. How had Ally managed to convince him of *that* so fast? They'd spent most of yesterday together and all of today. Had Jesse actually slept with her *last* night, after Morgan had given him the brush-off and gone into her room? Maybe that song really *had* been about Ally.

Because, while Morgan had thought Jesse had met her own eyes before he'd started singing it, Ally had been convinced he'd looked at *her*.

"Yeah, thought I would," he said. "Roof's done and all. No reason to stay, I reckon."

Her heart began to hurt. Badly. She covered over pain by manufacturing a sudden disgust. Only with Jesse would this happen – that two women would on the same night be convinced he was singing a song for them! And now Ally had him in her clutches, because she wasn't conflicted like Morgan. She wasn't confused. She knew what she wanted, and she was going to get it.

"I see," Morgan said frostily. "Well, thanks for everything!" And she wheeled and went into her room.

20

Early the next morning, Morgan was up and dressed well before dawn – she hadn't slept, anyway – and, when she went into the living room, the couch was empty.

She'd guessed Jesse would've gone upstairs to sleep with Ally, but seeing the evidence made her sick in her stomach and slightly dizzy. She shook her head clear, went to the mudroom and put on her coat, then hurried out the back door into the cool, damp morning, reminding herself of what was important. The contest. She had to somehow, somehow, all morning long, pretend that Ally wasn't the enemy. She had to be the most pleasant hostess ever, cook the best lobster on toast in the world, and win the $10,000 so she could install private bathrooms and make sure Woods and Water didn't steal her whole business along with her breakfast ideas. She'd gotten distracted these last few days with Jesse, but the Seacoast B&B was where her life was. Her real life.

She was just going to have to forget how Jesse had made her feel, how it had been to sing with him, the nights they'd spent together. The sense of comfort the first night. The ecstasy the second.

She was going to have to stuff her heart back inside her chest, zip it back up, and go on, and that was that. It was all for the best. The thought of her going to Fayetteville at all, or the dream of him staying on the island, was just crazy – even if he could get out of his obligation to his dad's business, imagine him surviving a winter out here! Or kowtowing to her guests all summer long (that was a laughable thought). Or playing endless gigs at the Barnacle, with nowhere else to go from there.

He would never be happy or satisfied, and he'd end up resenting her; hating her, even.

She'd known better than to dream, but she'd done it anyway. Now she was going to pay the price.

The moon was still shining on the water when she got the two shiny black-and-pink lobsters Tim Sawyer had left on the dock for her in a bucket, and she hurried back with them crawling over and around each other inside it. She grabbed four ears of corn from the garden, brought everything into the kitchen and got busy.

"Everything is just so *fresh*," Ally said, scraping the last kernels of corn from her plate. "It's amazing. I think that is the best lobster I've ever eaten." She smiled. "And I probably shouldn't say any more than that."

"I'm glad you enjoyed it." Morgan had been keeping her cool on the surface, but inside she was a roiling mess of questions. Jesse hadn't come downstairs yet, and Ally hadn't said a word about him. "And you slept well?"

"Oh, like a dream!" Smiling, Ally pushed back her chair. "Is Jesse available to help me get my bags down to the dock?"

Morgan was puzzled. Why wouldn't Ally know where he was? "I'm sure he is."

Just then, Jesse came in through the French doors, carrying his tool bag, with his duffel and guitar case slung over his shoulder. "Thought I heard my name being taken in vain out here."

"Oh, we wouldn't do that, Jesse," Ally said, giving him a flirty grin.

He grinned back. "Now, today's your lucky day, Ally, because I'm gonna ride with you all the way to the mainland. You all packed up and ready? I might have to take two trips for all this darn luggage."

"That is *great* news, Jesse," Ally said. "Let me just run upstairs and get my things."

"Some help down with those big suitcases?"

"Sure, thanks!"

And up the stairs they went, him following her a few paces behind.

Clearing the table, Morgan was completely confused. If Ally didn't even know Jesse was leaving with her, if Jesse hadn't spent the night with her last night, then what was going on? Where *had* he spent last night, and *why* was he leaving with Ally?

In a minute, they were back down. "Morgan, I can't thank you enough for everything," Ally said, coming over to shake her hand.

"Me, too," Jesse said. "Hope you don't mind, I slept in one of your extra rooms last night, since you said I could."

"Oh! Oh, that's no problem!" This piece of information clunked into place with the rest, and Morgan wished she knew what Jesse was thinking. Was he just *that* mad that she'd left the Barnacle last night?

"Ally," Jesse joked, "I hope you made notes on the comfy, comfy beds in this place."

"I certainly did."

"Aren't you hungry, Jesse?" Morgan said. "There's lobster for you."

"No, thanks."

She suddenly felt so hurt that she couldn't say a word.

Jesse slung his duffel and tool bag over his shoulder and picked up Ally's two suitcases. "If you carry my guitar, Al, I think we can do this in one shot."

Getting her wits about her – he was actually leaving! – Morgan broke in, hoping her panic didn't show. "I can walk down with you, carry something."

"Don't worry, we got it," Jesse said, not meeting her eyes.

Ally perched her sunglasses atop her head and picked up Jesse's guitar and her tote bag. "Thanks again, Morgan! You'll be hearing from me."

"Thanks, Ally!" Morgan said, following them to the door. "Jesse, can I talk to you for a second?"

He stopped and turned, and his eyes were the coldest she'd seen them. "What?"

Her courage faltered; she mustered it again. "Jesse, I'm sorry about last night," she said, speaking low so Ally wouldn't hear. Still, she had no idea what to say. "I just needed a little time to think…"

"It's no skin off my nose," Jesse said, and everything about him seemed closed off. She found she could say nothing more, as he turned away and walked out. Her heart screamed inside her chest. *It's for the best, it's for the best,* her brain consoled it. But even her brain wasn't convinced.

"Bye, Morgan!" Ally said, following him out into the autumn morning. The sky and harbor were gleaming blue, and trees were orange flames against it. Jesse didn't look back.

"Wait!" Morgan said, but only Ally turned, a smile on her face.

"What's up?" she said. Jesse, loaded down with luggage, was still walking away, and he was surely out of earshot by now.

Morgan folded her arms to keep everything from spilling out. "Have a good trip back. Come again."

"Thanks, Morgan, I will!" Ally turned to follow Jesse toward the dock.

The house felt as quiet as death. Morgan started cleaning, scrubbing down the whole kitchen then heading upstairs to strip the beds where Ally and Jesse had slept – separately. Even the evidence of *that* made her stomach hurt. How could she have been so wrong, last night? And for Jesse to leave just because she hadn't said anything right away about that song just didn't seem like him. More like him would've been to come after her and insist she talk to him. Had she just pushed him past his limits with all her uncertainty?

She tried to tell herself it didn't matter; that the time with him had been an interlude, after all. Her next guests arrived tomorrow, and she'd be right back on the treadmill of her real life, taking care of people, cooking breakfast and cleaning, at least for the weekend.

Tonight, though, she'd be absolutely alone in the house. She did not want to think about how that was going to feel. She could hardly stand to pass through her living room or look at the couch where she and Jesse had been together just a couple of nights ago. To try to fill the silence, she got Pandora playing on her computer – contemporary bluegrass, no country, since she didn't want to be reminded of Jesse.

She was just throwing a load into the washer when the phone rang. She went over by the computer to answer it. "Hello?"

"Morgan, it's Ally."

"Ally? You're breaking up a bit." Morgan turned the music down.

"Sorry, I'm on the road back to Portland. Can you hear me? I'm afraid I have some bad news."

"Are you all right? Is Jesse?"

"He's fine! I left him in the parking lot back there. No, I was just talking to Rob, my editor. I was telling him all about my visit with you, about those amazing apple-rosemary crepes yesterday, and he said he's been keeping an eye on a real up-and-coming place there on the island through B and B dot com, and that they just served those earlier this week, according to their reviews."

Morgan pressed a fist to her mouth, her stomach roiling. *How? How did they get a hold of that recipe?*

"It's terrible to have to say this, Morgan," Ally went on, "but Rob says we have to disqualify you."

The news fell on her like a ton of bricks. So she really was going to lose everything. Everything.

All her hard work had been for nothing, all her struggles the past few weeks – and so had Jesse's. Not to mention his whole trip up here.

Somehow, that made the whole thing feel even worse. "They've been stealing my ideas! All of them. I don't know how they got this one."

"I'm sorry, Morgan. I really am. I – " The line went dead.

"Ally? Ally?" Panicking, Morgan hit redial. The call went directly to Ally's voicemail. "Ally? It's Morgan. You must have gone through a dead zone. Call me back! I need to explain what's been going on." She hung up.

Right then, Pandora started a new song. Morgan recognized the opening chords of "Whenever You Come Around," then Allison Krauss started to sing.

"You have got to be kidding me!" Morgan said, and she clicked the sound off. Then she covered her face with her hands and cried.

*

21

Speeding down Route 1 somewhere in the wilds of Maine, driving faster than he should have, with the windows down so the cold air blowing in would keep him awake, Jesse wished he had a cup of coffee. He also wished he wasn't already behind schedule, especially when he had such a goddamn long way to go.

At the ferry dock, after saying goodbye to Ally – she'd given him her cell number, but he didn't plan to use it – and watching her tool away in her rental Jetta, he'd called his dad and said he'd be home by tomorrow night. That was before he'd turned the key in his truck's ignition only to find that nothing happened. He'd had to find a guy to give him a jump, and at least an hour had gone by before he got on the road.

Now he hit the Scan button on his radio and cursed. With his old antenna, he could hardly get a single station to come in. He hit it again, and a loud voice came on: "Maine's Number One Country!" Good. Perfect. An old tune by Tracy Lawrence, "Lessons Learned," came on, and Jesse sang along as he squinted against the sun, watched the autumn-colored trees skate by, and did his best to muster enthusiasm about going home. At least there, life was real, as Morgan put it. He understood the terms that people operated under. He knew not to hope for too much.

Then from his speakers came the opening chords of "Whenever You Come Around." He cursed again, but listened to Allison Krauss sing the first couple of lines.

Then the memories of Morgan at the campfire hit him too hard, and he slammed the radio's power button. "Give me a goddamned break," he said out loud, with the wind the only sound in the cab.

He tried singing to himself, but all he could think of were the songs he'd written while he was on the island. *Shadows on my heart, waitin' on the stars....* Right. He was going to be waiting forever on that one, he guessed. The whole time out there might as well have been a dream. Or, an "interlude," as Morgan had called it.

Yet, he already missed the place. And he missed *her* more than he could really stand.

Suddenly, he heard a loud thunk. The truck wobbled, veered right. Blowout! He clutched the wheel with both hands and steered through – he'd been through this before – giving a little more gas until the truck was under control. Then he braked gradually, downshifting, and got himself steered onto the shoulder.

Heart pounding, he shut off the truck, took a deep breath, and cursed again to himself. A tire must have gotten low while the truck was sitting there at the dock all that time. Could things get any worse?

Morgan's face flashed in his mind, the way she'd looked at him that night they'd spent together. Traffic whizzed by. He watched in his mirror and waited for a break, then climbed out. He walked around the hood to the passenger side. Sure enough, the front tire was totally fubar.

Still feeling shaken up, really wishing now for that cup of coffee, for a chance to sit down and get his bearings, he walked around to the back of the truck and crouched to pull the spare tire out from under the bed.

The spare was flat, too. Yep, things could always get worse.

"You're telling me," Morgan said, standing on the front porch of Woods and Water, glaring at Mr. DuPage, "you have *no* idea how your breakfasts just got magically better in the last four weeks? And you didn't know that you'd gotten expelled from SIBA? And you haven't seen the flyers posted all around town?"

The man shook his bald head. "My wife doesn't let me set foot in the kitchen, mornings, and I haven't been to town in days. I've been working on a new painting and it's keeping me involved night and day. And she certainly never said anything to me about SIBA." He smiled brightly. "Though the leftovers I've sampled have been outstanding. She said she's been doing research."

"Research. Right. I bet she has. I need to talk to her."

"I'm sorry. She meditates in our garden during the lunch hour. She can't be disturbed."

"We'll just see about that," Morgan said, and she turned and ran down the stairs and around the side of the big house.

"Wait!" Mr. DuPage said. She could hear him puffing as he followed her. "She doesn't like to be interrupted!"

In the backyard, Morgan let herself in the garden gate. Under the shelter of tall cedars and pines, the garden was huge and lovely, with shade-loving perennials – small, because they were new this year – turning to their fall hues of brown and gold and orange. In one sunny swath, Black-eyed Susans swayed in the light breeze. Clearly, no one was growing any food here, and Morgan couldn't help feeling scorn about that.

She hurried down the path, looking in all the nooks and crannies, at all the benches and seating areas, for Mrs. DuPage. The woman was nowhere in sight. Morgan stopped, listening to the wind in the trees. There was a sense of peace here that she liked – at least until Mr. DuPage came up beside her. "Now, that's very strange. She must have gone to the store instead."

Nothing was working out like Morgan had planned. She needed to go home, figure out what she could possibly do about the disaster that was her life. "You tell your wife I'll be back to talk to her," she told him, and she turned and walked away.

She called Ally again, and this time Ally answered. But when Morgan explained everything that had been going on with Woods and Water, Ally sounded skeptical. "I don't know, Morgan. It isn't that I don't believe you. It's just that uniqueness is one of the main factors in the judging, and that's been seriously compromised in your case. I mean, if you're collaborating with that other place, or somehow franchising with them…"

"I'm not collaborating with them; I just told you! What if I came up with another new idea to replace the crepes?"

A short laugh. "What are you going to do, FedEx it to me? I don't have time to come back. In fact, you've pretty much wasted my time already."

Between the lines, in the tone of her voice, was her disappointment that she hadn't gotten farther with Jesse.

Morgan took a deep breath. "Ally, listen, I'm telling you, I'm being sabotaged here. I put everything I had into this, and more. Please, give me another chance."

A pause, then a sigh. "I'll talk to Rob, see what I can do."

"Thank you, Ally!"

"Bye, Morgan." The line went dead.

Morgan guessed she could go see Lainey for moral support, but she was in no mood to rehash terrible events. She sat down at the computer and went to an online forum for B&B owners. Without using her name or going into specifics, she typed a query asking for suggestions of how to handle a competitor who was fighting dirty. Waiting for comments, she scrolled the list of other topics. One from a few days ago said, *Nashville area B&B for sale.*

She clicked on the link and read the listing. *Financially viable small inn only ten miles from downtown Music City!* The pictures showed a charming old white house with a big front porch, four large guest rooms with private bathrooms, tastefully decorated living and dining areas, and a fabulous gourmet kitchen. *Owners' quarters with three bedrooms, including a gorgeous master suite! Large, established kitchen, herb, and flower gardens.*

Suddenly, Morgan felt so hungry that she was absolutely starving, almost to the point she couldn't stand it. She never felt hungry! But now she just *had* to eat. What would be quick to make? What did she want? *Not* the lobster she'd made for Jesse – that would only remind her of everything that had gone so wrong.

She got up from the desk and, blocking out thoughts of the contest, of all the recipes ideas she'd gone through, worked with, tossed out, and made in the past several weeks, she started to mix up a batch of pecan waffles. The kitchen was too quiet, so she went back to the computer, started Pandora again and chose "The Lumineers" station, where she figured there'd be almost no chance of any song that reminded her of Jesse to come on.

Not that she needed a song to remind her of him.

She plugged in the waffle iron, and, by the time she'd finished the batter, chopping the pecans fine, the iron was hot. She poured batter over the griddle and watched the creamy stuff spread and fill in the gaps, then closed the lid and got out the maple syrup to heat it. The second the waffle was ready, she slapped it onto a plate, poured warm syrup over it, and began to eat. Sweetness exploded in her mouth, and tasted so good that she ate without pause until the plate was clean. Then she poured more batter on the iron, dropped the lid, and watched the steam impatiently.

She repeated the process three more times before she started to feel full.

Still, she was a long way from satisfied.

As she cleaned up, she remembered Jesse: *When are you going to start thinking about what you need?*

From the computer came the beginning of song she recognized like the back of her own hand: The Cowboy Junkies singing "Blue Moon Revisited." She used to sing it with her band and she used to sing it to Rick when they were alone. The last night she'd had with him, at their little house in Wilmington, he'd put the CD on "repeat" and they'd danced to it in their tiny living room for at least an hour, holding each other and breathing each other in like they were already dreams to each other.

Now she let that memory and the music wash over her, dancing around her kitchen with her own arms wrapped around herself. Tears streamed down her face, but when the song finally faded out, she felt a bit lighter, more free. She also felt something tremendous and unsettling happening. "Rick?" she whispered. "Are you leaving me? Please, don't."

The computer started to play "Whenever You Come Around."

"Seriously?" She wiped her face and laughed. "Seriously, sweetheart?"

But, as she listened, leaning back against the counter where, just days ago, Jesse had come so close to kissing her the first time, she thought of singing with him the other night, "Go Rest High on that Mountain," how her tears had streamed then, too. With Jesse was the first time she'd really faced her loss. She'd been living all this time trying not to feel pain, but pain had defined everything she'd done, the entire way she'd conducted her life. She'd spent so much time taking care of other people, feeding other people, that she hadn't even noticed *she'd* been starving.

At least until Jesse showed up, and showed her all the ways life could be bigger and better and more full. More real. In real life, you *felt* things. You needed things. Food, a warm touch. Sometimes you had to cry, or laugh, or get mad and shout and scream. And sometimes, you could actually feel, for a moment or two, complete.

Suddenly, a sense of immense comfort came over her. And a sense of certainty.

So much so that the song was only half over when she clicked it off, picked up the phone again and dialed. "Lainey? Would you come over, please? Hurry. I need to talk to you."

Then she went into her bedroom and looked at the display on the dresser devoted to Rick. She touched the glass covering their wedding picture. She opened the wooden box with the cards inside and stacked the two bundles of ribbon-tied letters in there, too. Then she took the ring off her finger, kissed it, and put it in the box, too. "Thank you, sweetheart," she said, resting her hand on the closed lid. And then she did feel him leaving her, and she cried until she couldn't cry anymore.

Then she went into her closet to look for her suitcase.

22

By the time the guy from the garage Jesse'd managed to locate through his phone showed up with a new tire, Jesse already had the old one off. Burt, according to the name stitched on his shirt, shook his head at the sight of the bare rim, seeming to take Jesse's effort as an insult. "Now, that's part of the service you're paying for, designed so you don't have to lift a finger."

"I didn't mind a bit," Jesse assured him. "Just want to get back on the road."

But even with all the traffic zooming by, Burt seemed as unphased as a man taking all day at his golf game. As he got the new tire on the rim and began tightening the lug nuts, he started asking Jesse everything under the sun: where he was from, if it was still warm down there, where he was heading back from, how he'd liked Seacoast, and on and on. Then, noticing Jesse's boot tapping on the asphalt, he chuckled and said, "You're in such a hurry, you must have a girl waiting back home."

"Not exactly," Jesse said, and he couldn't help picturing Morgan again.

"Ah ha," said Burt, pausing his work to look up. "So you're leaving one behind up here. You met someone?"

Jesse laughed. This guy was unbelievable. "It's complicated."

Burt went back to the lug nuts. "Listen, in matters of the heart, there ain't nothing complicated. That's just an excuse people make when they chicken out. Do you love her?"

The nerve of this guy! But somehow Jesse found himself answering. "Yeah. I think I do." He'd written it in his song, after all.

"That's a bullshit answer," Burt said. "You do or you don't."

Jesse thought of how he'd felt when he was with her. "All right. Yeah, okay, I do. I sure as hell never expected to!"

"Now we're getting somewhere. And does she love you?"

Jesse laughed again. "Who *are* you – some kind of internet preacher or something?"

Burt gave a slow smile. "Let me tell you, son, a man that changes tires hears more tales than a bartender or a priest. When you're vulnerable on the side of the road, and a lot of times you've just seen your life flash before your eyes, and seen how short life can *be*, well, that's when the truth comes out. That's a fact. And I've been doing this for years." Burt moved on to the next lug nut. "So, what's the deal? You might as well get the most out of this roadside service." He laughed at his own joke.

Jesse didn't laugh. He *did* know how short life could be. Of all people, he *should* know. And Morgan should, too. "Well, I don't know if she does. Love me. That's the problem." He explained about Rick, about the display on Morgan's dresser.

"So you just left. Real smart. So how do you think your buddy would feel about you falling in love with his wife, and her with you?"

Jesse thought about it. Cars whizzed by. The wind rustled in nearby trees. Burt's torque wrench clicked as he made the last lug nut just tight enough. "Well," Jesse said, "he told me once that if anything ever happened to him, he wanted her to be happy. And one other time we were talking about that same subject, he asked me to take care of her."

Burt patted the new tire and creaked to his feet. "These old bones," he lamented. "So, you ever heard that saying, 'All's fair in love and war'?"

"Sure."

"Seems to me in your case nothing's been fair about either. But, in my humble opinion, you can't let that keep you from your own chance at happiness."

Jesse hadn't told Burt how he was pretty sure Morgan had just used him for sex.

Except now he started to wonder. She really had seemed to struggle with the situation, those few days before they'd fallen together on the couch. She'd said over and over they should just be friends. She'd also said she was powerfully attracted to him and that she admired him, too. Was there a chance that she'd gone ahead with him because she'd just gotten overpowered by her feelings, same as he had?

And was there a chance she'd acted so odd about Ally and run out of the Barnacle last night not because she didn't have feelings for him, but because she *did* and they scared her?

Because if she'd gone without sex for six years, it was pretty foolish – and arrogant, really – to think that suddenly she'd needed it so badly she'd use him, of all people. Especially when they'd already agreed that having sex would screw up a friendship they both valued.

"I've always believed in gray areas," he told Burt. "I guess I forgot that, here, lately. You think she could love me even though she still loves him?"

"I surely do think it's been done. That'll be one-ninety, please, and I *can* take a credit card. Got that little doo-hickey for my phone." Burt grinned.

Back on the road, Jesse turned on the radio again and tried not to think too much. Burt had been disappointed that Jesse wasn't turning around to head back in Morgan's direction, but Burt didn't understand how Jesse's dad was counting on him to be back in Fayetteville in time to go to work Saturday morning and how Morgan probably didn't want to see him at all. Besides, he was still licking his wounds, which were raw after last night and this morning.

And, if he went back, what would he say to her, anyway? Even if she wanted to be with him, it wouldn't be fair to expect her to give up her business and her whole life on the island. His vision of love was of a family and a home and being together through thick and thin. Between his obligations in Fayetteville and hers on the island, that seemed a bit out of reach.

The traffic was terrible. Who *were* all these people, and where did they come from?

That's right, Morgan had said that a ton of "leaf peepers" and retirees showed up in the fall, especially on the weekends, and here it was Thursday, which evidently was close enough.

He couldn't help thinking about her, continuing to go through the motions of feeding and housing people – every weekend up through New Years', she'd said. It made him lonely to think of her doing all that by herself; to think of not being there with her.

At the thought of the sound of her voice blending with his, his heart pinched.

He was doing the right thing, right, continuing to drive away?

Yes. For one thing, she was probably too elegant for him. He'd always more figured he belonged with girls with big hair.

Someone honked at him, and he moved into the right lane, even as he realized that, with those girls with big hair, sex had always been something slightly mechanical. Various parts involved, but not his whole self.

With Morgan, his entire body, head to toes, had not only been involved, they'd all felt suffused with a warmth and ecstasy he could only think – especially after his conversation with Burt – was love.

To be able to love someone with every fiber of your being, wasn't that what everybody, deep down, hoped for?

Besides, Morgan only *seemed* elegant. In fact, she was way more like him than anyone would see at first glance: she worked hard every single day, grew her own food, changed her work according to the seasons… Besides, her favorite way to express herself was – if she let herself – to sing her heart out.

Anyway, he liked an elegant woman. Always had. He just hadn't necessarily believed himself worthy of one.

He thought of that contest and wished he hadn't left before figuring out who the Woods and Water mole was and giving him a good pounding.

What kind of "friend" was he, anyway, leaving without things like that being resolved? Leaving without *anything* being resolved, actually. He could practically see Rick, shaking his head with that disappointed look he used to get when one of his men didn't live up to standard.

We can't all live up to you, buddy, he told him.

You can try, Jesse'd have sworn he heard back.

He shook his head, fiddled with the radio dial. The station he'd been listening to had gone to static, but he quickly found a different country station. He was in Portland now; a blue bay shone in the distance over the rim of the freeway, and gold and orange trees were all around. Slow cars moved through crowded lanes, everyone changing like that would get them where they were going any faster. If traffic was like this all the way through New England, he'd be lucky if he got to Rhode Island tonight, especially since, the way things were going, he was on pace to be in Boston around rush hour.

He sighed at the thought. An old song by Wade Hayes, one of Jesse's favorites, came on the radio.

It somehow reminded him of Rick, one night after Jesse'd played for the guys, saying, "Man, you have *got* to go to Nashville when this shit is over. You're *good.*" And, when Jesse had objected: "Nope, I won't take no for an answer. I'm going to hold you accountable, dude. Ac-*count*-able."

So, after Rick died, why had Jesse kept avoiding it? Signed on for another four years? If he'd really been a good friend, wouldn't he have gone to Nashville to try to make it in Rick's memory?

Nope, he'd served four more years instead. And then – in what even his dad, who needed him at home, admitted was kind of a bonehead move – retired *now*, after only fourteen years in, which meant he was six years short of getting a pension.

He didn't exactly know why he'd done it; it wasn't like he had a long-term plan. He was just plum tuckered out, in his body, mind, and heart. Besides, he'd managed to sock away quite a bit of pay from all his time overseas, and he'd told himself he'd be just fine.

But the truth was that money wouldn't last long. If he bought a house or a little farm, like he wanted to, that would pretty much take care of it.

Which meant he'd pretty much consigned himself to a life pounding on roofs with his daddy.

He guessed he'd been figuring, up till recently, that that was A-Okay. At least he was still alive.

And it was hard to think, sometimes, that much in life meant very much, after seeing the things he'd seen.

Yet, with Morgan, he'd managed to forget all that. Everything had seemed to mean *a lot*. Even a piddly contest for some magazine. Getting that roof done.

Making her smile.

He remembered Rick, when Jesse teased him at his wedding about having won the lotto. "Someday, man," Rick had said, and the look in his eyes had been intense. "Someday, you'll get this lucky, too."

Surely he hadn't meant with the very same woman.

Man, sometimes life just straight up wasn't fair. Like Jesse'd told Morgan, he didn't understand why *he'd* made it home to his fairly pointless life, when Rick, who had so much to live for, hadn't.

Then, on the radio, "Whenever You Come Around" started to play again.

Tears came to Jesse's eyes. "Jesus Christ, man, you don't let up," he said, wiping them away. He turned up the volume and, giving in to all his feelings, everything he remembered of Morgan and everything he hoped for, he got the message: Life wouldn't be pointless if he loved her. If he made her smile every day. If he gave her the life that she deserved, the children she wished for. Put some of that money he'd saved to the good use of *giving* her a good life, one where she wouldn't have to work so blessed hard all the time.

And, if he did all that, it suddenly seemed clear, he'd have everything *he'd* ever wanted and needed, too.

In the face of all that, the conflict about where they'd make their life seemed small. They could talk about it. Figure it out. He didn't have to have the answers right now. All he needed to know was that he loved her.

And he needed to know that she loved him, too.

On the radio, "Whenever You Come Around" was winding down. "Okay, okay, buddy," Jesse said out loud to Rick. "I get it. But you can't be hanging around all the time, all right?"

He could almost hear Rick laughing, and then his presence was suddenly gone.

Jesse felt like his eyes were open wider; like he could see more clearly. He was sad, but he was free. And things finally, finally, made a kind of sense. He shut off the radio, took the next exit, and somehow found his way around the maze of roads to come back out on the other side, heading north again.

23

Morgan ran all the way to the dock with her suitcase and pounded up the ferry's ramp just seconds before the crew pulled it in. "Made it!" she said, and the crewman loosening the lines grinned, as if her optimism was contagious.

After Columbus Day weekend, only one ferry ran per day the rest of October, and it left at 3:30. By the skin of her teeth, she'd gotten everything done in time: arranged to borrow Brick's car to drive herself from the dock to the hotel she'd booked in Portland; arranged for Lainey and Hannah to take care of the guests scheduled to arrive tomorrow; bought tickets for tomorrow for the Portland to Boston bus and a flight from Boston to Fayetteville; and packed a suitcase full of everything she needed – plus, as Jesse would say, some "actual clothes."

If all went according to plan, she'd touch down in Fayetteville tomorrow night at ten, about the time Jesse should be arriving, too. Then she'd rent a car, call Jesse, and let him know she was coming to see him, wherever he was.

If that failed, she'd somehow figure out where his father's farm was – and go there and wait.

And if Ally called to say *Simple Food* would accept another recipe in exchange for the compromised apple-rosemary crepes, *Simple Food* would have to understand that Morgan needed a little time.

Some things were just more important than others, she'd learned. Too bad she'd had to watch Jesse walk away in order to realize it.

"The good thing is," she'd told Lainey, "now I'm sure Rick would be okay with it. That he *is* okay with it. I mean, I've been getting so many signs I'd have to be blind not to see. Does that sound crazy?"

Lainey grinned. "All I know is, there's no doubt you'll get Jesse back. You have a plan!"

"Not an actual plan, so much as a hope-for-the-best-and-jump! It's slightly crazy, right? Jetting off to Fayetteville like this? And thinking of heading off to Nashville at this point in life? If I can even convince him to take the chance? Not to mention convince him to leave his father's business! Are you sure you won't hate me forever if I leave?"

Lainey smiled at the rush of questions. "Well, I don't *want* you to leave. I was going to wait till after I'd been to the doctor to tell you, but... you're going to be an aunt! Or, well, you know, an honorary one."

Morgan squealed and hugged her. "Oh, my God, Lainey, I knew it! How far along are you?"

"About eight weeks, I think. I had to swear the staff at Island General to secrecy when I bought a test. I'm going to the doctor this week."

"Oh, boy!" Then Morgan couldn't help frowning. "Well, this changes things. I want to be here for you. I mean, I wouldn't miss it for the world."

"Don't you dare not go after him." Then Lainey grinned. "On the other hand, if you could convince him to move out here, I know Brick would give him a job. He keeps talking about how he wants to."

"But imagine Jesse out here in the winter. He gets so cold."

"Just find him. Talk to him. I'd hate for you to leave, but I also want you to be happy," Lainey said, and, with that, they hugged each other hard.

Now, as Morgan leaned on the rail catching her breath and the ferry burbled away from the Seacoast pier, she didn't have any idea what her future would hold.

But she knew how Jesse had felt about her as recently as last night. All she had to hope was that telling him tomorrow that she felt the same – and that she thought together they could figure out a way for *all* their dreams to come true – wouldn't be too late.

Two hours later, with the sky and water turning pink and the air getting frosty, Morgan wrestled her suitcase into the trunk of Brick's black BMW, a vestige of his former life in Boston that he hadn't found the heart to give up.

All the other ferry passengers had had someone to meet them, to help with their things and whisk them off in a warm car, and here she was, as always, struggling with things by herself. She sure was tired of that, and as she slammed the trunk shut, her optimism was wavering. She stood looking out to the midnight blue water and the island she could just make out in the distance beyond.

Even if she found Jesse tomorrow, what would he say? And was she really ready to give up everything she'd built here and start a new life with him? She loved Seacoast so much. It was hard to imagine living anywhere else – despite everything that had happened with Woods and Water to push her over the edge this morning and make her consider a different life.

A loud motor caused her to glance around to see who was disturbing the stillness in the near-darkness. An old Ford pick-up. She turned back to the BMW, fishing in her pocket for Brick's key, before she realized that the driver of that truck had been a handsome man in a beat-up straw cowboy hat with the brim turned up.

She turned, pressing a hand to where her heart was climbing up her throat. The truck pulled into a parking spot opposite Brick's car. The engine shut off, then the lights. The only sound was the water lapping the pier.

Jesse stepped out of the truck. The door slammed, a metallic echo.

He turned, glancing around at the nearly deserted lot, a look of frustration on his face.

Then he saw her, and, even at that distance and in the dusk, Morgan could see his eyebrows shoot up. Her toes curled inside her boots.

His head cocked to one side. Then, slowly, a smile spread across his face, and her fears lifted off her, and happiness swarmed in.

He ambled toward her, grinning. "Well, well. Look who's standing here looking like a million bucks and then some."

She grinned back, though she wished she'd done more than throw a sweater and a jacket over her regular outfit – she'd planned for better once she got to Fayetteville. "You still haven't learned to wear a jacket?"

"Heat was on in the truck," he said, coming closer.

She looked up at him. He didn't look like he was mad anymore about her running out of the Barnacle last night. In fact, he looked just as relieved and happy to see her as she was to see him.

"Heat's on over here, seems like," he said.

She blushed, smiling still, but didn't break his gaze.

"Where you headed?" he asked. "In this little ole BMW?"

Everything just felt *right*, now that he was here. As always, his eyes implored her to tell the whole truth, and she reveled in the safety and delight of that. "It's Brick's car. I'm heading for the airport. I've got a ticket to go to Fayetteville."

He let out a long whistle. "Now, that's a distance. Fayetteville? Why on earth would you want to go there?"

This was no time for holding back. "I'm in love with a man who lives there. I'm hoping he might love me back... at least if I tell him I want to be in a relationship with him."

Jesse's smile was broader than she'd ever seen it. "Is that so?"

She reached out, then, and touched his beautiful face. "Jesse, I'm sorry – "

He grabbed her hand and looked at it. Her left hand, the ring finger boasting a white tan line, the ghost of where that gold band had been for so many years. He looked up and grinned. "Why, Morgan Bailey."

She soaked up the warmth that was in his eyes as he looked at her, letting it warm her all through. "I think he wouldn't mind," she said. "I think he'd want us to be happy."

"I was getting that same idea."

She couldn't help smiling again. "You came back."

"Now, I hope you won't be getting on that plane to Fayetteville. There's not some other relationship-happy fella down there, is there?"

She laughed. "I think I'll be canceling that ticket."

He took another step closer and put his hands inside her open jacket on her waist. They were warm and wonderful and she wanted to lose herself in his touch.

But so many questions had been swirling through her mind all day, and some problems still felt nearly insurmountable. "What about your father, Jesse?" she asked.

He kissed her lightly. "Seemed to me like the best thing to do was to get back here, and let the rest work itself out."

"Jesse, you don't think I'll disappoint you?"

"I don't think you ever could."

It was the best thing he could have said. "Jesse, I've been thinking."

He kissed her lightly again. "Yeah?"

She was hungry for him, but she made herself keep talking. "Do you think that people in Nashville need to have a lot of roofing work done?"

He pulled back an inch at that, just quickly, then he laughed and picked her up and set her on the trunk of

Brick's car, and even though the metal was cold through her jeans, she was warm everywhere else. "I imagine there's some call for it, Mrs. Bailey."

She loved his strength, his nearness, everything about him. "You have to stop calling me that," she said, wrapping her legs around his waist, her arms around his neck.

"What are you cooking up now, Morgan?" he said, and she kissed him till they both saw stars.

A few minutes later, when Jesse got cold, she used his cell phone to call Lainey, whose number she knew by heart. Lainey called Tim Sawyer at home, and Tim got on his radio to find out if any lobstermen were still out. Going to a hotel wouldn't have been the worst thing, but Morgan wanted Jesse in her own bed, for the first time. Everything would seem more real then, and she needed that.

Lainey called Jesse's phone to report that Caleb Brown's grandson would be there in thirty minutes to get them. He was out late trying to catch up on hauling his grandfather's traps.

Jesse laughed, shaking his head. "Man, I don't know what I was thinking – that I could just show up and find somebody to take me back?"

"You were optimistic," Morgan said. "Anyway, now I'm here. To keep you warm."

They huddled together at the back of Caleb's boat among the lobsters, holding hands. Caleb's grandson was tall and good-looking in a dark wool cap and orange fishing overalls over a heavy sweatshirt. The dark beard that was growing in didn't mask his strong jawline. "Name's Caleb Rayford," he'd said, his smile shining in the darkness. "People on the island call me Rafe, so my grandpa doesn't confuse me with himself." He laughed at his own joke.

"How is your grandpa?" Morgan asked.

"Ornery as the devil, but I think he'll survive this one. But, man, this island really needs an emergency response team. I mean, what if Tim hadn't been close by?"

"We do have the emergency water taxi," Morgan said.

"Yeah, but nobody dedicated to driving it. Just a volunteer list of guys who generally are all out fishing all day."

"Seems like everybody watches out for everybody pretty good out here," Jesse put in.

"Yeah, but still. There need to be systems in place." Rafe shifted the boat into high gear and the diesel responded.

After that, it was too cold and noisy to talk much. Morgan hadn't said any more about Nashville, and Jesse hadn't asked – maybe they were both a little afraid to talk about the future, when even the present was so tenuous, so new. Plus, the more she thought about it, the less she wanted to leave the island, especially given Lainey's news. And now that Jesse had come back, she guessed she was hoping maybe he liked it here more than she'd thought.

Quiet and happy, they hurried back to the B&B, with him carrying her suitcase and his guitar and duffel, and got inside as quickly as they could. They didn't make it past the mudroom before they were kissing and touching and unraveling the mystery of each other's clothes, and only with one last determined effort did she get him into her room and her bed, and in the darkness they were heat and light together.

Afterward, they lay together breathing, letting their bodies melt and cool at once. "You," he said happily.

"You," she said back.

He laughed. "Man, this bed is *comfy*," he said, pulling the down comforter up over them, now that they were cooling down. "To think we could've been in here all those nights you had me out there on the couch..."

She shoved him playfully, kissed him again.

He twined his hand with hers, looking again at the white space on her finger. "You okay, really?"

"I'm okay. Yes." Then she laughed. "Better than okay. You're here."

"Look, I know I'll never be... him – "

She shushed him with a kiss. "I don't want to hear you talk like that. Ever."

He smiled. "Okay, then."

Satisfied, she lay back. "Lainey's pregnant. She told me today."

"Hey, isn't that exciting! Just like you thought." He kissed her.

Somehow, though, thinking of Lainey made Morgan remember the state of things as she'd left them here, imagining as she had that she wouldn't be back for a few days, at least. At the thought of dealing with the whole Woods and Water scandal again, she sighed.

"What's wrong?" Jesse said.

"I just remembered. Stupid, really; it doesn't really matter, now that you're here. But Ally called and I'm going to be disqualified from that contest. Woods and Water served my apple-rosemary crepes earlier in the week."

Next to her, Jesse stiffened. "How'd they manage that? Nobody knew about that but you and me. And I sure didn't tell anyone."

"I don't know. I talked to Mr. DuPage today and he swore he didn't know anything. Mrs. DuPage was out, and I was just so discouraged I gave up for the moment. Figured I had more important things to think about. You, for example."

He kissed her quickly at that, then wrestled with the covers, swung his legs away. She missed his heat immediately. "Where are you going?"

Jesse was reaching for his jeans. "Are you kidding? Up there to get some answers. It's high time someone did. You worked too hard to get disqualified by some goddamn squirrel."

24

Morgan got dressed, too, and she and Jesse hurried up into the woods, following a flashlight beam.

They ran up Woods and Water's porch steps, and Jesse pounded on the front door. No answer. He pounded again. Finally, Mr. DuPage answered, looking perturbed, a paintbrush in his hand.

He shook his head at their questions. "I'm sorry, Morgan. She was so upset when I told her about your accusations that she went out this afternoon and I haven't seen her since. I'm starting to get worried, frankly." He didn't look worried, though. He looked like a man who was enjoying having time to himself to paint. He glanced at his watch, and his eyebrows shot up. "Oh, dear. It's even later than I thought. Nine thirty." He poked his nose outside. "And it's cold."

"We'll look for her," Jesse growled, and Morgan felt lucky he was on her side. "Don't you worry about that."

Mr. DuPage smiled, evidently happy he didn't have to venture out. "Well, okay. Try the Cutthroat; she goes there some nights for a drink. Or maybe she's out meditating in the garden again, though that's hard to imagine with it being so cold." He shrugged. "Anyway, if I haven't heard from any of you in an hour, I'm calling Jack Harrison." In lieu of a police or fire department, people tended to call Jack when there was trouble.

"You can bet we're going to locate her," Jesse said.

Mr. DuPage laughed merrily and shut the door in their faces.

At that, Morgan had to laugh, too; the whole situation was so ridiculous, and she was just so happy that Jesse was there, that they were really going to try to make it work, even if they had no clue right now how they would. Jesse grinned, too, and grabbed her hand, and together they set off to look for Mrs. DuPage like it was some grand adventure.

"We might as well look in the garden first, while we're here," Morgan said, still holding back giggles. "She could have built a fire or something. Or she could have a space heater in that little shed." With the flashlight lighting the way, they walked around to the back of the house. There was no evidence of a campfire, but they hadn't gone far before they heard an odd cry.

"What is that? Coon?" Jesse said.

Morgan snickered. "Armadillo, maybe."

"Shh!"

They listened. It came again. More of a moan this time, but the same tone, so likely the same creature. The noise was coming from the area of the little garden shed. Jesse pointed the flashlight and they crept nearer.

Another noise, in a different tone.

"Sounds like she's got *some* kind of heater in there."

Morgan shoved his arm. "Smartass."

"Sure, but you love me."

She grinned. "Yes, I do." They paused to kiss. Another noise interrupted them.

Jesse pointed the flashlight again. They followed the beam to the garden shed, and it was clear the noises were coming from inside. A low moan in one voice, a gasp in another.

Jesse looked at Morgan, raising his eyebrow in a question.

She nodded. Whoever was in there with Mrs. DuPage was obviously the mole. The cause of Morgan's ruin. She was in no mood to respect the pair's privacy, when they'd had no respect for her at all.

Jesse pulled on the door. It must have been latched from the inside.

The noises stopped. Morgan held her breath.

Jesse yanked hard and the door flew open, metal parts of a latch or hook flying and scattering on the pathway's stones. Morgan was treated to the sight of Mrs. DuPage's back, and then it came clear the woman was straddling someone who, seated under her, tried to hide his head behind her shoulder. Both of them were dressed, thank God, and her skirt covered up what was going on underneath, but Jesse's flashlight on the side of the man's pale leg left no room for doubt what that was. Then Jesse pointed the beam at Mrs. DuPage's shoulder, which couldn't hide the spiky red hair behind it.

"Uriah!" Jesse said. "The one who was always pointing us to somebody else. And maker of the best burgers on the island at the Cutthroat. Shouldn't you be at work right now?"

"This is an outrage," Mrs. DuPage said over her shoulder, ignoring the position she was in. "Bursting in on private property this way!"

Jesse gave a short laugh. "Moral outrage doesn't fly too well when you've got your knickers over your head, Mrs. DuPage. Besides, your husband asked us to look for you, said you might be in the garden, so I guess that gives us the right to be here. What do you think he'll have to say about this?"

"Oh, my husband!" Mrs. DuPage said, climbing off Uriah, leaving him scrambling to turn around and button his pants. Mrs. DuPage straightened her clothes and stood with her arms folded, as if she were the one being wronged. "My husband thought it would be a great idea to run a B&B in 'our next chapter.' 'Early retirement.' Ha! More like a way to keep me out of his hair – what little he's got. Said he was *sure* I could learn to cook, no problem, and we'd hire the rest. Too bad he hates people! Spends all day working on his precious paintings, and acts like everything from the cooking to the accounting to the reservations just magically gets done! Not to mention he doesn't notice me – *me!* – and I could dance naked in front of him and he wouldn't look up from his goddamn palette. He doesn't care one iota what I do. Well, I'll tell you, sometimes you have to make your own magic, and I won't apologize for that."

Morgan broke in. "Uriah, how could you? And, anyway, how did you? You're a short-order cook. You figured out my recipes from tasting them once and recreated them?"

Uriah ran an angry hand through his angry shock of hair. "I went to the fucking Cordon Bleu, Morgan. Last year. Would've graduated top notch only someone sabotaged *me*, made it so I got kicked out for poor conduct."

Mrs. DuPage rolled her smoky eyes. "And your attitude now is so peachy."

Uriah glared, then clearly decided he wasn't going to take the fall alone. "So Patty and me got to talking one night at the Cutthroat and she made me an offer I couldn't refuse. Stuck all summer making goddamned hamburgers, right? I was bored out of my skull. So I got to do a little fine cooking, and I got to do her." He smiled.

No one else did. Patty just rolled her eyes again.

"So why did it have to be *my* recipes?" Morgan said. "Why didn't you make up your own?"

He shrugged. "I never was a breakfast guy. And, I mean, you made it so easy, that dopey tasting group you had. Besides, once I started it, she got off on it." With a slight nod, he indicated Patty. "Said she wanted to drive you just crazy enough and drive you out of business, just so you'd end up coming to work for her so she didn't have to make her pitiful attempts at cooking anymore. Anyway, she said nothing I could come up with would be as good as yours, but whatever."

Mrs. DuPage huffed. "I will not listen to such accusations."

Morgan ignored her and turned back to Uriah. "So, how did you get that last one? The apple-rosemary crepes. Nobody even knew about it."

"Ah, well, Morgan." Uriah sighed. "You shouldn't have left your empty house unlocked and your notes in plain sight in the kitchen drawer."

Her heart pounded. "When?"

He shrugged. "Guess it was Saturday."

"Karaoke night at the Cutthroat," Jesse said, his voice was full of regret. "When I got you and all your guests to go."

Uriah shrugged. "Yeah, so I saw you all there, and on my break I came over." He pointed to Patty. "*She* wouldn't give me anymore unless I gave *her* some more. If you get my drift." And then he smirked and rested his case.

"Can you believe that?" Morgan said two hours later, in bed. She'd just finished canceling her ticket to Fayetteville, and since it was within 24 hours of when she'd purchased it, she got the whole amount back, which was great, though as long as Jesse was here she wouldn't have cared about forfeiting the money.

Now, though, at almost midnight, the day was catching up with her, and she shivered. "They weren't even sorry." Uriah had held his head up even as the islanders were leading him to Tim Sawyer's boat. Tim had agreed to make an extra, late-night trip to the mainland. The weather was clear, and everyone from Lainey and Brick to Jack Harrison agreed Uriah shouldn't spend one more minute on the island.

"It's all right, baby," Jesse said, pulling Morgan close. "I think good ole Mr. DuPage is going to make *her* sorry, at least. I heard him yelling as we left that he'd done all this for her, built this place, he thought she liked it, how could she, and so on. Seems he actually does care what she's up to, even if she didn't think so."

"At least it's over now."

"You think Ally and her editor will give you another shot, let you submit another recipe?"

Morgan got nervous, suddenly, and realized she wasn't ready to propose her idea about Nashville yet. Or her idea of seeing if Ally and Rob would stay silent on the Seacoast B&B debacle this year and let her enter a Nashville B&B in next year's contest.

What if Jesse thought she was crazy? What if he insisted he had to go back to live in Fayetteville?

The last thing she wanted to do tonight was fight.

She twined her leg around his. "Let's not think about that right now," she said, and kissed him.

25

In the morning, after Jesse brought Morgan coffee and scones in bed ("Are you kidding me?" she said, laughing and laughing, kissing him and pulling him down so she almost spilled coffee all over the sheets, and fortunately he caught the tray in time and set it aside before climbing between those sheets with her), he told her he needed to go talk to Brick. He left her lolling in bed both pouting and looking as relaxed and happy as he'd ever seen her.

But when he got over to Wildflower Books & Wine, it was Hannah he actually wanted to see.

Last night, driving back north again, all he could think about was getting close to Morgan again, trying to make her understand how he felt. Then, he'd been so blown away by finding her at the dock on her way to see *him* that he hadn't put a single thought to the future, he'd just reveled in the present. He'd called his dad yesterday from the truck and told him he wouldn't be coming back just yet, but he'd told him he would come back soon. *After* he'd figured out how to make things work with Morgan. His dad had actually seemed happy about that, though he did grumble a bit about how much work was waiting for Jesse.

Now, though, Jesse was thinking of making his time in Fayetteville into a short-term deal. Morgan had mentioned Nashville last night, and if she was really that serious about making things work with him that she'd consider giving up life on Seacoast, well, he wasn't about to let that sentiment pass by without cementing the details as quickly as possible.

Fortunately, Hannah was in the shop inventorying the wine, and she stood from her crouch, tossed her dark hair, and smiled. "Heard you came back last night," she said, and when she saw his look of surprise, she added, "Word travels fast out here."

"Guess so! Anyway, I don't guess I could take a look at some of those rings you've got for sale? Like the one you showed me? And then you could pretend I never did any such thing, so the story doesn't get around to everybody before I get the chance to talk to *her*?"

She grinned and led him to the small case in the corner of the wine room where she had her wares displayed. "This is the one," she told him, her eyes lighting up and her face softening as she pulled out a delicate silver ring with a single glimmering pink stone. "The stone's called Morganite. Symbolically, it stands for joy. Calm. Good things, basically. And, you know, the name's right, right? It's pretty much the most engagement-y ring I've got, anyway. I don't work with diamonds or anything."

"It's perfect. I'll take it. How much?" Jesse said, and pretty soon he was walking out of the shop with it in his pocket in a little box, whistling.

Morgan was nervous about talking to Jesse about the future, but when she checked her messages after getting her three pairs of weekend guests settled in, there was a message from Ally, not saying what the verdict was, only asking for Morgan to call her back.

So if Morgan was going to try to convince *Simple Food* to visit her in Nashville next year, she guessed she'd better introduce the idea to Jesse.

He wasn't back yet, though. She was hungry again and decided to make BLTs. She was just finishing them when Jesse walked in. "Oh, my Lord, bacon." He wrapped her in a bear hug and planted a kiss on her forehead. "Morgan Bailey, you make me the happiest man in the world."

She grinned and kissed him, finishing up the sandwiches. She handed him a plate with two on it, and she took her plate of one, and they sat down together at the counter. It was just like old times, in a way, only a thousand times better, because now she knew she could look forward to, she hoped, endless meals with him well into the future.

If only she could figure out what that future would be.

He kept his hand on her thigh under the counter and ate his sandwich one-handed, which she loved.

"You and Brick must have had a lot to talk about," she said, fishing a little. Was there any chance Jesse would have been talking to Brick about a job?

He grinned. "Yeah."

Just then, Lainey burst into the kitchen, smiling broadly. "Hey, you two, good news! I just saw Jack

Harrison down at the Post Office, and he said Mr. DuPage kicked Mrs. DuPage off the island and he's shutting down Woods and Water! Kaput, that's it. Shutting it down and putting it on the market. He's so disgusted by what she did, he hired one of the guys to take her to the mainland this morning."

"Well, and we didn't even have time to give her a farewell party," Jesse drawled.

"Wow, that's amazing," Morgan said wanly, because her plan for the future would depend on someone buying her B&B – and, if Woods and Water went up for sale, any potential buyer might go for it instead.

"Jack said Mr. DuPage wants to give *you* a special deal on it, Morgan," Lainey said. "Maybe you should go up there and talk to him." She grinned at Jesse. "I'll see you two later. Hannah needs help at the shop. She's had a *very* busy morning." With one last bright look at Jesse, she turned away.

"Great, see you later," Morgan said, and Lainey was gone.

"Well, that's good news," Jesse said, polishing off his second sandwich. "You've ousted the competition."

Morgan couldn't hold in her thoughts any longer. She set down what was left of her BLT. "Jesse?"

"Yes?"

"You know what I said last night about Nashville? About all the roofs that might need work?"

He grinned. "Yes."

The grin seemed like a good sign, and encouraged her to go on. "Well, here. I've been thinking. Come over to the computer with me."

She took his hand and led him the short distance to the computer. He sat down and she perched on his lap, and he wrapped his arms around her waist. He was sturdy and strong, and nothing had ever felt so right. "I figure, we only live once, right?" she said, as she opened the page showing the Nashville B&B. Her heart was pounding. "I just found this listing yesterday. And I was thinking, if I owned this and we lived there, and I cooked and we gardened and maybe hired some of the other work done, and you worked on roofs during the day to bring in extra money, and we tried to get gigs at night... You know, we could see how goes. At least our dreams of making a go of it with music would have a chance."

He grinned. "You're resurrecting that one for yourself, huh?"

"I guess I am!"

"Wow, when you say you're ready to get into a relationship, you don't do halfway."

She laughed. "I'm not scaring you off, am I?"

He shook his head, held on a little tighter. "It means the world, all of this. But the thing I *don't* want is for you to have to work as hard as you've been working all this time. I want your life to get easier, not harder. That place looks really big, and it would be busy all year-round, right? So you'd never get a break. Besides, this is your home. You don't really want to leave, do you?"

As Morgan tried to think what to say – because, truth be told, she *didn't* – there was a brief knock at the front door, and she heard it open and shut. Then Mr. DuPage walked into the kitchen. Looking around, he clasped his hands in front of his chest. "Oh, yes, this would do nicely!"

"Excuse me?" Morgan said.

He grinned. "Here's my proposal. You buy my place for a dollar, and I buy this place from you for a dollar. If I open it up to other people at all, it'll be as an artist's retreat, not a bed and breakfast."

Morgan couldn't believe what she was hearing. "What?"

Mr. DuPage shrugged. "That place has bad associations for me now. And it's clear you're the one cut out for that line of work. Besides, the light's no good up there. This place would be ideal for painting. Anyway, I'm giving Patty the house in New Jersey. She won't complain. She never liked it here. Me, I want to live here year round and *paint*." He looked thrilled at the thought. "It was what I wanted to begin with, only I thought she needed something to keep her busy." At the thought of what she had *found* to keep her busy, his face clouded over. Then he caught himself and grinned again, like he was free. "What do you say?"

Up at Woods and Water, Morgan, still in a daze, followed Jesse up the stairs, holding his hand. Mr. DuPage had told them to take a look around. "Take as long as you like! Leave no stone unturned! I think you'll find it to your liking."

Indeed, the guest rooms were lovely, with large windows looking out at the trees. For Morgan's tastes, they'd need redecorating – there was a little too much onyx and gold – but that was something she would love to do. As for the fixtures and the furniture, no expense had been spared. Three of the rooms had whirlpool tubs, and all had beautiful bathrooms, comfortable sitting areas and huge beds.

She and Jesse were both speechless as they went back downstairs to check out the big dining room, which had a lovely window that looked out onto the garden. But when they went into the kitchen, Morgan couldn't hold in an "Oh, my God."

It was the most beautiful kitchen she'd ever seen, with a huge island, high-end gas range, and a double oven *plus* a convection oven. "Two dishwashers," Jesse said. "Guess that would come in handy. And check out the view of the garden. We could clear a section for vegetables, in that sunny spot back there."

Morgan, who'd been doing all her dishes by hand all these years with a view of nothing more than a lilac bush, was speechless.

"Let's check out the owners' quarters." Jesse led her through the door on the other side of the kitchen. They found themselves in a beautiful family room with a big TV, comfortable leather couches, and a dining table on the side closest to the kitchen. The whole room was lined with built-in bookshelves, and, again, big windows looked out on the garden.

At the front of the house was a more formal sitting room, with a bay window looking out over the front porch. Morgan and Jesse climbed another set of stairs to the second floor and found a gorgeous master bedroom with a balcony overlooking the garden. "We'd have our own whirlpool!" Jesse said, peering into the master bath.

Moving down the hall toward the front of the house, they found another full bathroom and two more bedrooms. The front bedroom had big windows looking out at the woods and was set up as Mr. DuPage's painting studio.

"Wow," Morgan said. "Just, wow."

"I'd say jump on this deal before he comes to his senses!" Jesse said.

"Wow," Morgan said again.

"That kitchen alone," Jesse said. "You'd be in heaven." Then he nudged her. "Besides, there's room for a family here, unlike your place. I mean, just looking down the road. This room right here would make a pretty good nursery, right?" He smiled.

At that, though she couldn't quite wrap her mind around *everything* he was saying, Morgan finally regained the ability to form words. "What about you? What about Nashville?"

"Well, here. I've got an idea. I've saved up money to buy a house, right? So what if I bought a little house in Nashville?"

She frowned. "I thought we were going to try to make this work."

He laughed. "You didn't let me finish. So, obviously, this deal is too good to pass up. Forget buying that B&B in Nashville when you can get this one pretty much for free, right?"

She nodded. Much as she loved her little place, she'd be crazy to turn down this opportunity. She could really expand – and cooking in that kitchen *would* be heaven. Plus, she wouldn't have to leave Seacoast.

"Okay," Jesse went on, "so what if the new and improved Seacoast B&B, formerly Woods and Water, is only open from, say, June to October? No more fooling with weekends and holidays. And you and I work our tails off all summer here, then we go to Nashville for the winters and have a good time singing our little hearts out."

The idea struck her as so wonderful that she grinned. No more lonely, long winters. Singing with Jesse. Building a life with Jesse. And still living on Seacoast part of the year. "And see what happens?"

"That was kinda my idea. Thanks to you thinking of it first."

She laughed, then quickly sobered with another thought. "But are you sure you can get away from your father?"

"It's been done before, I reckon. He might be torqued off, a bit, but he didn't seem displeased when I said I was in love with you."

"You told him that?" She was thrilled.

Jesse nodded. He moved close and put his arms around her. "Anyway, my dad wants me to be happy, I'm pretty sure of that. I might have to go help him with this big job the next couple-three weeks, 'cause he took it thinking I was going to be there, and I don't want to leave him high and dry. After that, he can sell the damn business and buy himself a condo in Florida and a damn sailboat if he wants to. I don't care about getting a legacy. Long as I got you."

She grinned, wrapped her arms around his neck and kissed him.

"Wait, wait, wait," Jesse said, turning away.

"What now? Are you always going to keep me from kissing you?"

"That is not my plan. However, right now, there's something in my pocket jabbing me. Maybe you could just reach right in there and take it out." He nodded down at the front of his pants.

"Jesse!" She laughed, then slid her hand inside his jeans pocket. There was a hard, square object in there, and she managed to get a hold of it. "What is this? Or are you just happy to see me?" she joked.

"I'm always happy to see you."

She laughed, wrestling a little box out of his pocket. She recognized the logo on top. Hannah Champlain's *Silver Star Designs.*

"So *where* did you go this morning?" she said happily.

"May have gone on a small errand."

"Can I open it?"

"Wish you would."

She lifted the lid off the box. Resting on cotton inside was a beautiful little ring.

He reached down and, with two big fingers, picked up the little thing. "Why, look at that." A pink stone glimmered in the light.

"Jesse?"

He took her left hand in his, held the ring with his right hand, and sank to one knee. "I don't want to just undertake all this and 'see how things go.' Okay, Morgan? I want you to marry me. I want us to be a family. Thick and thin. Better or worse. The whole part and parcel. The whole kit and caboodle. You know?"

"Oh, Jesse. Yes. Please. Yes."

He slid the ring onto her finger, and her heart swelled with love. He stood to kiss her, and all was right with the world.

When they finally stopped for breath, he laughed a little and kissed her nose. "Anyway, thought if we were going to start doing our damndest to make some babies to fill up all these rooms, I ought to make an honest woman out of you."

She laughed, shoved him a little, kissed him again. "I love you, Jesse Stewart."

He grinned. "That's right, I guess we skipped that part. I love you, too. A whole heaping lot, let me tell you."

"I think I knew it from the first moment you stepped off that boat."

"Me, too. Goddamn. Only, what, three weeks ago?"

"A lot has happened."

His hand crept to her breast. "Then again, we've got some lost time to make up for."

She laughed. "Oh, but if I'd've slept with you right away, you never would have respected me."

"If I'd've slept with *you* right away, you never would have respected *me*. Wasn't I the one to put the brakes on, that first time?"

She laughed again, pressing as close to him as she could. "Oh, Jesse. Life with you is never going to be dull."

"Promises, promises," he said, leaning in to kiss her neck, making her melt, making her want to feel his skin on hers.

"So, you want to go tell Mr. DuPage we're gonna go for it?"

"Yes, let's."

"What are you going to do about that contest? Ally and all?"

"Maybe I should see if they'd withdraw me from this year's contest and visit me – visit us – again next year. I was thinking of trying that with the Nashville place. Why not try it here?"

He nodded in approval. "Sounds like that'd be good for business. Our business."

She loved the sound of that.

She was just about to kiss him again when his hold on her tightened another degree, and he cupped her head in his big hand and pressed his cheek to her hair, like just maybe he was a little overwhelmed by all that had happened. She loved him even more for his vulnerability. "I'm never going to let you go, baby," he said. "Never, never, never." He let out a quick sigh. "Goddamn it, we're lucky, you know?"

"I know," she said, leaning in to him, too, knowing he was thinking of Rick, and that Rick would, in some ways, always be a part of them. And wasn't that one of the luckiest things of all, when you came right down to it? That they got to love each other, who had each known and loved Rick so well? "I know."

That night at the Barnacle, everyone was there to celebrate, because news had spread the way it always did around the island – fast – and Morgan and Jesse sang and sang, and everybody cheered them.

Morgan had talked to Ally, and Ally had convinced Rob to print that the Seacoast B&B had withdrawn from the competition due to extenuating circumstances. Ally was excited to hear about Morgan moving up to Woods and Water, and said she hoped she'd be able to come back the next year to judge Morgan's cooking again. "I mean, honestly, you would've won, Morgan. I'm glad these jerks who were taking advantage of you are ending up making it up to you by giving you such a great opportunity."

As for the news about Morgan and Jesse being engaged, Ally was flabbergasted. "I never guessed, the two of you? Gosh, I'm sorry, I never would've tried to talk to him if... you know... if I knew."

Morgan was so happy she only laughed. "It's all right, Ally, *we* were confused, so there was no reason to expect that *you* could've known what was going on."

Jesse had talked to his dad, who'd agreed that, if Jesse would come back and work for him for the next three weeks, that would be enough time to finish the project in progress and figure out what to do over the winter. He said he couldn't wait to meet Morgan, and he hoped that she and Jesse would come to spend Thanksgiving or Christmas – "or both!" – with Jesse's whole family.

"Boy, things could not have worked out any better!" Lainey said, when Morgan and Jesse finally got down off the stage and joined their friends at their table. "Even if you go away for the winter, maybe you'll be back by the time the baby comes. That should be April, by the way."

Morgan grinned and kissed Jesse's cheek. "We've got a lot to figure out, but I don't care. I'm so happy. I mean, depending on when we can get the deal finalized, maybe my weekend and holiday guests will just have to upgrade to the new facility!"

"I'm trying to convince her to cancel them," Jesse said. "Seeing as how she just pretty much won the lottery."

"*We* did, you mean," Morgan said, and they grinned at each other.

Just then, Caleb Rayford came up to their table, a beer in his hand. "Hey, Morgan, Jesse. I didn't realize when I gave you a ride last night that I was transporting the next American Idol act. Johnny and June, here."

Everybody laughed. Morgan introduced Lainey and Brick, then asked Rafe, "How's your grandpa? I've been meaning to bring him some food, but today was… well, a little crazy." She laughed again, in happiness.

Rafe shook his head and whistled, but he was smiling, too. "Like I said, ornery as the devil. I had to get out of there for a while."

"How long are you going to be staying on the island?" Brick asked.

"A couple months, from what I can tell right now."

"You're trained as a paramedic, right? That's what I heard."

"That's right."

Brick nodded, looking satisfied. "That's good. My wife's pregnant, and I'm not sure about the wisdom of being out here all winter."

"Brick!" Lainey said. "We're going to be just fine. We talked about this."

"I'm just saying, I'm glad somebody with some medical training is going to be around."

"Well, congratulations," Rafe said. "And, yeah, call me if you need anything. If I haven't strangled my grandpa by then and got put in prison, I'll be glad to help out." He laughed, toasted them with his beer and moved on.

"So I'm supposed to put my life in *his* hands?" Lainey said, arching an eyebrow at Brick, who shrugged.

"He seems nice," Morgan said.

"Morgan, you're so happy, you'd think Dracula was nice right now."

Morgan laughed. "That's true!" She kissed Jesse again.

"Me," Jesse said, "I'd think Cruella DeVille was a princess." He grinned.

Hannah came up and pulled up a chair. "Who was that you all were just talking to? He's *cute*. And so *tall*."

"I thought you were nearly engaged," Jesse teased.

"Doesn't mean I can't look. Congratulations, by the way. Now, spill."

"That, my dear," said Lainey, "is Caleb Rayford, Caleb Brown's grandson."

Hannah made a face. "Oh, the lobsterman. Right. Okay, well, guess it's still all-systems-go to go back to New York. Anyway, he probably only looks good because the light's so dim in here."

Morgan laughed. "You're such a snob, Hannah."

"That is the cross I'll have to bear," Hannah said with a giggle, "while I'm attending the ballet and eating in the finest restaurants all winter long."

"Speaking of fitting in around here," Jesse said. "I'd like to make an announcement." He cleared his throat dramatically, and everyone waited. "Okay, here's the deal. I love this woman, Morgan Bailey, and, even though she made me work like a son-of-a-gun to install a goddamned cedar shake roof, I'm going to marry her at the first possible chance. First possible chance, I'm telling you! And we are going to live happily ever after in our big new house on the hill and our little old house in Nashville, which is the player to be named later in this deal. That and the babies we're planning to have." He grinned. "Just wanted to clarify."

Morgan grinned back and kissed him. Everyone else was smiling, too, and Brick said, "We already knew all that, buddy. Haven't you heard? Word travels fast around here."

MORGAN'S APPLE-ROSEMARY CREPES WITH CRÈME BRULÉE SAUCE

For the filling:
2 T. butter
3 medium tart apples, such as Granny Smith, sliced thinly
½ c. dried cranberries
1 T. cinnamon
1 T. finely chopped fresh rosemary
Pinch of salt
Melt butter in large skillet and sauté apples and cranberries with spices, stirring frequently, until the apples are tender.

For the crepes:
1 c. flour
1 ½ c. milk
2 eggs
1 T. melted butter
Pinch of salt
Sift together flour, sugar and salt; set aside. In a large bowl, beat eggs and milk together. Beat in flour mixture until smooth; stir in melted butter.

Add approximately ¼ c. of the batter to a lightly buttered pan preheated on medium. Carefully tilt the pan in a circular motion to distribute the batter into a thin crepe. Cook until lightly browned (about 2-3 minutes), then gently flip using a spatula and cook until brown on the other side.

For the sauce:
1 ½ c. granulated sugar
2 T. water
¾ c. heavy cream
½ t. vanilla extract
1 t. cinnamon
Using a wooden spoon, combine sugar and water in a large saucepan over a high heat, stirring constantly. Use a dampened pastry brush to brush any stray sugar particles off the sides of the pan. Continue to stir until mixture forms a caramel-like mixture, dark amber in color. Remove from heat and gradually add cream, stirring briskly after each addition. Add cinnamon and vanilla and return to the heat for one minute. Keep stirring,

and make sure you don't leave the pan on the heat any longer.

When ready to serve, divide the filling evenly among the crepes, then roll the crepes into tight cylinders. Pour the sauce immediately over the filled crepes. Garnish with fresh rosemary leaves and freshly whipped cream.

ISLAND WINTER

A Seacoast Island Romance: Volume 3

COMING IN MARCH 2016

Hannah Champlain always thought she'd be just a summer person on Seacoast Island – until she discovered her Manhattan boyfriend in bed with her Manhattan bestie. Now she's signed on to spend the winter – and tall, blue-eyed sixth-generation lobsterman Caleb Rayford bets her a thousand dollars she won't last through the battles with firewood, howling blizzards, and solitude.

But when Caleb's sternman is injured and Hannah's the only one available to fill in, community pressure means she rises to the challenge. Now her days are spent out on the churning, icy sea, hauling traps with Caleb, and each moment tests her mettle – and her resolve not to fall for the salty, handsome lobsterman who begins to hint that he might not mind losing that bet…

28723823R10160

Made in the USA
San Bernardino, CA
05 January 2016